The Dream Catcher

GREGORY BAIRD

The Dream Catcher

Cover design by Marianne Miller

ISBN 978-0-578-60942-3

Gregory Baird
deeperazure@gmail.com

For Marianne

I. A LONG TIME AGO

1.

He did not have long to live. The boy had seen the change in these last days. The Old Man, with all of his many secrets, would soon breathe no more.

The boy's heart was heavy. So much had the Old Man taught him; so much had he taught the whole tribe; so many times had the boy gazed into the Old Man's eyes and felt their radiant warmth, those eyes somehow all-knowing, all-embracing, always looking into the distance, or into the innermost part of one's soul. The boy loved the Old Man, as he had since before he could remember.

The sun was setting, and the boy followed the Old Man across the desert. The Old Man's steps were slow, but steady. They had been walking since morning, stopping occasionally to rest, the Old Man quiet in those moments, saying nothing, staring out across the flat. The boy was full of questions, but he knew not to ask them; the Old Man did things in his own way. But the boy felt sure about one thing: this was the day! The day he had waited for had come, the day the Old Man promised so long ago—the day of the Secret. And though he knew his feelings were childish, he felt proud that the Old Man had chosen *him*.

When they reached the butte, they began a slow climb up the stone cliffs. The sun was down now, and the full moon had risen in the east, casting long shadows across the sandstone. Why were they climbing? Where were they going? He struggled to contain his excitement. Everything around him seemed to vibrate and shimmer in crystal clarity. The desert floor, now far below him, glowed in the moonlight, brighter tonight than he had ever seen it. The night breeze was cool on his face. His body felt light. He felt if he let go of the cliff he would soar like an eagle, his arms becoming wings of moonlight, catching drafts of warm air from the sand below hammered hot by the day's sun, wafting him gently up to heaven.

A rock suddenly came loose under his hand, jarring him out of his dreaming. It clattered down the rock face. The Old Man slowly looked back over his shoulder; his eyes met the boy's, and the boy smiled as if to shrug. The Old Man remained expressionless. They continued to climb.

As they neared the top, the boy noticed an opening in the cliff above them. It looked like the entrance to a cave. This surely was the secret place. A kiva in the sky. Above him, the Old Man disappeared into the dark passageway, and when the boy reached the entrance, he followed him.

A short time later, they stood face to face in the vast secret chamber.

"Many will come in search of this place," the Old Man said.

The boy's mind reeled. He could scarcely follow the Old Man's words. He did not understand where they were, like a cave but so strange.

"You must listen to me now," the Old Man said. "Soon I will be gone, and you will be alone with the knowledge of all that you have seen."

The boy steadied his thoughts. He looked into the Old Man's eyes and felt calmness and wisdom there.

"The Secret must be kept from them." The boy nodded slowly, and the Old Man continued. "You and those who come after you will be the guardians, until the time comes."

"Until what time?"

"You and those who come after you will dream of that time. And as you dream, so shall it be."

4

The boy closed his eyes and tried to understand. What was the Secret? How long must he guard it? How could he know what to dream? The questions raced through his head, but he really wasn't sure what to ask.

"Why?" the boy asked, finally.

The Old Man smiled, and the boy noticed something in his hands. It seemed to shine, to glow; it seemed angular, yet curved, solid, yet liquid. The Old Man offered it to him. The boy reached out, palms up. The Old Man placed the object in the boy's cupped hands.

And the world dissolved into webs of light.

The next day, on the flat tabletop of the butte, far above the valley, the boy burned the Old Man's body, as he had been instructed.

II. A FEW YEARS AGO

2.

It was a warm spring afternoon, and Matthew Wilkes was flying. Across the desert he soared. Down below him, some of the women were tanning skins; others were busy rolling flatbread between their hands and cooking it on hot stones. Matthew caught a whiff of the smoky corn aroma and was hungry. He glided over warriors crouched for the hunt, toward the caves, and saw the medicine man, surrounded by a small group of initiates. The medicine man, he knew, was the wisest man of the tribe. As he circled the small group, the medicine man looked up at him, smiled and waved. Matthew smiled and waved back.

Suddenly feeling a hand on his shoulder, he snapped out of his daydream and found himself looking up into the face of Mrs. Tilley. Matthew didn't like Mrs. Tilley. He liked their regular teacher, Mrs. Kline, but she was having a baby. He hoped Mrs. Tilley would have a baby, too.

"Daydreaming again, Matthew?" Mrs. Tilley asked.

"No, I was reading."

"Oh really? What about?" she asked, wearing one of those adult smiles for which Matthew had recently found the perfect word: condescending. It was a very condescending smile.

"The Hopi."

"Indians?"

"They're a Pueblo tribe in the American Southwest. They're very peaceful. They—"

Mrs. Tilley picked up the book from Matthew's desk. "Is this book on the reading list?"

9

"No, my father gave it to me."

She still had that smile. Matthew summoned up his best condescending tone. "And for your information, we prefer to call them Native Americans."

Her smile disappeared.

"Well, well, aren't we precocious," she said.

"Mrs. Kline usually lets me read on my own," hinted Matthew.

"I see. Well, go on then." She handed the book back to him and continued on her rounds.

Later, on the bus home, Matthew sat alone. The other children talked and sang and teased each other, but Matthew was never included. At least they don't tease me, he thought, though he often wondered why they didn't, since he seemed to himself to be the perfect target.

"I know about Native Americans, too, you know." A brown-haired girl leaned over the back of Matthew's seat. "Not as much as you, but more than the rest of these lamebrains." Matthew knew her name was Monica, and he liked her. He liked her ponytail and her huge brown eyes. She seemed to get along with everybody, which certainly impressed him. She's very friendly, he thought. Maybe that's why no one teased her.

"How come you read so much?" she asked. "You're pretty smart, aren't you?"

"I suppose so," Matthew said.

"See, that's what I mean. You don't say, 'Yeah, I guess so' or 'I dunno.' You say, 'I suppose so.' You're weird. You talk like a grown-up. What does your dad do?"

"He's a scientist."

"Figures," she said, nodding. "My dad's just a drunk. Oh, here's my stop."

Monica hurried to the front of the bus and bounded off. Matthew watched her through the back window of the bus as it pulled away. He hoped she would wave goodbye. She did.

"Am I weird?"

Matthew sat at the dinner table, his feet dangling above the floor. He was busy trying to make the solar system out of his dinner; the peas were the asteroid belt.

"Weird? Oh, I don't think so. Strange, perhaps, but not weird," said Mrs. Vines.

Dolores Vines had taken care of Matthew since he was three months old, for the more than eight years since the death of his mother. If Matthew had been her own child, she couldn't have loved him more.

"Somebody told me I was weird."

"Who?"

"Some girl."

"Oh, I see," said Mrs. Vines, suppressing a smile.

"I mean, kids don't seem to like me very much. Except for Monica, I suppose."

"Is she the girl who said you were weird?"

"She's the one."

"I see," said Mrs. Vines, knitting her brow as if puzzling something out. "But she likes you?"

"I think so."

"Even though she thinks you're weird?"

"True ... " Matthew thought about this for a moment. "Is Dad coming to dinner?" he asked, changing the subject.

"He's busy in his study, dear."

"Maybe I should bring him some food."

"I don't think he wants to be disturbed."

"I'll bet he's working on something exciting!"

"I'm sure he is," Mrs. Vines said. "Now, if you're finished playing with your food, I'd like to see you eat at least some of it."

"Okay." Matthew shoved some asteroids into his mouth. "Mmmm, delicious!" he exclaimed cheerfully, and it really was. Of course, he would have said it was even if it wasn't. He wouldn't want to hurt her feelings. He loved Mrs. Vines more than anything. Almost as much as he loved his father.

Later, Matthew lay in bed, watching tree shadows the moonlight cast in his room. He couldn't sleep. His father had been working in his study all night. He hadn't even tucked Matthew in. This could mean only one thing: his father was planning another expedition.

Matthew tried to imagine what it could be. Maybe his father was planning a jungle adventure . . . going deep into the jungle in search of . . . dinosaurs. Or maybe a cave—that was even better. Huge dinosaurs living hidden beneath the surface of the earth. Enormous subterranean caverns. Bottomless chasms. He let his mind wander . . .

Matthew got out of bed and went downstairs. The house was dark; Mrs. Vines, he knew, had long since gone to bed. But as he expected, there was light coming from under the door to his father's study. He tiptoed to it, turned the knob slowly, and quietly pushed open the door.

Matthew's father stood over a large map spread out on a table. The room was dark, lit only by a task light shining on the map and by the glow of his computer. With a compass and a ruler, he seemed to be plotting coordinates. He turned to his laptop and typed in some data, staring intently into the screen, his face lit by the glow. His concentration was intense; he didn't notice Matthew.

"Dad?" Matthew asked timidly. His father looked up, as if he had heard some faint sound far away.

"Dad?" Matthew said again. Now his father looked at him, but he seemed confused, still lost in thought. After a moment, though, he smiled.

"Oh, it's you. I didn't see you there." His father stretched as if waking from a nap. "So, is it time for dinner?"

"Dad, it's three o'clock in the morning," Matthew said. His father looked at his watch.

"So it is. I guess I was working so hard I just lost track of time."

"That's for sure!"

"Which, of course, doesn't explain what you're doing up at three in the morning, young man. It's Tuesday night, and I think you're going to be a little tired at school tomorrow."

"It's Friday, Dad."

"Hmmm," his father said, pondering this new information. "Then I guess the only logical thing to do is to have some ice cream."

"Are you working on something exciting, Dad? Are you going on an expedition?"

"Could be," his father said with a grin.

"Could I come? I wouldn't get in the way. I could even help. I'm pretty smart these days, you know. Ask my teachers."

"Get over here," his father commanded, playfully scooping Matthew up in a big hug. "You're about the smartest person I know, and someday, when you're a little older, we'll have an adventure together. If you're still interested, that is. But first you've got to help me answer an age-old question."

"What's that?" Matthew asked, wide-eyed.

"Rum Raisin or Rocky Road?"

3.

"There! I know it's right there!" Jonathan Wilkes said, thrusting his finger at the map. The old professor pursed his lips.

"Ridiculous!"

It was a familiar situation. Over the years they'd had many such meetings in the oak-paneled office at the university: Jonathan, brash and full of passion and enthusiasm; the professor, older and wiser, cast in the role of the skeptic.

"Jonathan, my boy, why can't you give this up?"

"Because of the chance I'm right."

"Nonsense," the old man said gruffly. He tamped his pipe and lit it. Smoke billowed around his head as he puffed.

Professor Theodore Schnabel was the grand old man of the anthropology department, author of a dozen books, veteran of twice as many major expeditions, and one of the most beloved teachers on campus. Jonathan had been his best student. He knew Jonathan thought of him as his father, and he, in return, felt a father's affection. Never having been blessed by children, Jonathan was the closest he would ever come to having a son of his own.

"You yourself always said that most myths have a basis in fact," Jonathan said, resuming the attack.

"I never said that!"

"You're worried about me, aren't you?" asked Jonathan.

"Balderdash! I'm just trying to save you from wasting your time."

"The worst that can happen is that I come back empty-handed, realize I was wrong, and find out there's no secret to be discovered after all. At least I'll know I did my best."

The old professor shook his head. "You and your wild theories. Why can't you be like my other students? Why can't you study something . . . normal?"

Jonathan smiled. "First of all, I haven't been your student for quite a while. And secondly, you love me just the way I am."

"Bah!" snorted the professor, sitting back in his chair. Jonathan folded his map. The old man frowned.

"What about Matthew?" the professor asked.

"He'll be fine with Mrs. Vines."

"What if something happens to you out there? You have responsibilities, you know. You can't just go gallivanting all over creation."

"I have to. You should know that better than anyone. Wasn't it you who said, 'There is no higher calling than science'?"

"I never said that," the professor grumbled. Jonathan smiled. They both sat quietly for a few moments.

"So you're going?"

"Yes, sir."

"You're just going to ignore all the wise, level-headed advice I'm giving you?"

"Yes, sir."

"Anything I can say to change your mind?"

"No, sir."

"Well then, I have only one thing to say." The professor puffed thoughtfully on his pipe. "Good luck, my boy."

Over the next several weeks, Jonathan prepared for his trip. Except for Professor Schnabel, he told no one where he was going, or why.

This really is a crazy notion, he thought at times. *If I'm wrong, nobody needs to know.*

And Jonathan knew there would be no danger. Just a hike in the desert. Hadn't Mrs. Vines said he needed a vacation? When he thought along these lines he became cheerful, whistling happily to himself while he packed his gear, studied his notes, planned his route. He read to Matthew from books about dinosaurs, astronomy, and Native-American cultures. Matthew had shown an increasing interest in that last subject, and he was pleased to teach his son about one of his own areas of expertise. The Hopi seemed particularly fascinating to Matthew, as if he somehow sensed the nature of his father's trip.

As the day of his departure drew near, however, Jonathan began to feel a strange apprehension. When had he developed this theory, anyway? he wondered. He couldn't remember. He found himself seeing it all from Professor Schnabel's point of view. It *did* seem crazy, didn't it? The stuff of science fiction, of fantasy, like crackpot notions about UFOs, ESP, or the Loch Ness Monster. But what disturbed him the most was not the possibility he was wrong. It was that, with as much certainty as he'd ever known anything in his life, he *knew* he was right.

"Where are you going, Dad?"

"On a little trip, that's all."

"Far away?"

"Not far."

"What are you looking for?"

"Oh, this and that. Nothing important. I'll be back in a week or two."

"Is it dangerous?"

"Not at all. Don't worry about me. You just take good care of Mrs. Vines."

"I will. Be careful."

"I will."

4.

It was nearly a month later when Mrs. Vines sat at the kitchen table, hearing the news that the search had been called off.

"To be honest, ma'am, I don't think they're going to find him," said the man with the police. "They've searched the area indicated by Professor ... uh ..." —he glanced at some notes—"Professor Schnabel. There's no trace of him."

"Oh my," was all Mrs. Vines could say. She pressed her hand over her mouth. The man continued to speak, but she heard only bits and pieces: "... anywhere out there ... anything could have happened ... might never find the body ... " She was thinking only of Matthew. Her eyes filled with tears. She would cry now and get it over with. Then, no more tears. She would have to be strong for Matthew's sake.

"Does the boy know?" This time, the young woman spoke. Mrs. Vines knew she was some sort of social worker.

"No. I'll tell him tonight."

"Is there a next of kin?"

"His mother died when he was a baby," Mrs. Vines said. "The grandparents are all gone. He'll stay with me."

"It's not that simple—"

"Professor Wilkes made all the arrangements. I was to be his legal guardian if something were to happen..." Her voice trailed off. Poor boy, she thought. How he loved his father. She took a deep breath and looked the young woman in the eyes.

"The papers are with the lawyers," Mrs. Vines said curtly.

"I see," said the young woman. "Then, assuming that's all in order, I'd say Matthew's lucky to have you."

At the top of the stairs, hidden in the shadows, Matthew felt relieved. He'd been afraid they would take him away from Mrs. Vines. Now he knew it wouldn't happen.

That night, Mrs. Vines told Matthew his father was gone.

"He'll come back," was all Matthew said.

In the months following Jonathan Wilkes's disappearance, Mrs. Vines was greatly concerned about Matthew. She found him a therapist and took him twice a week.

"This kind of denial is not uncommon," the therapist told her. "It may continue for some time, though. But eventually he will accept the truth."

After a few sessions, the doctor's prediction came true. "My father's gone," Matthew would now say when asked about him. The doctor was satisfied, and Mrs. Vines stopped taking him, satisfied, too, that Matthew understood his father wouldn't be coming home. There remained only her lingering concern that Matthew had still not shed a single tear.

III. SEVEN YEARS LATER

5.

Being fifteen years old was not easy for Monica Jordan. For one thing, the changes in her body seemed to her like the onset of some sort of disease. She was no longer "one of the boys," no matter how hard she tried to act like one. And as for the girls, their boy craziness made her sick, and all the girly dresses and earrings, the constant texting about hair and nail polish, were horrible. Particularly because it seemed to work. The boys ate it up.

She responded to all of this by wearing baggy jeans and oversized flannel shirts, and by bullying as many boys as she could get her hands on. (She was still stronger than most of them, though that, too, seemed to be changing.) They're all sheep, she thought. Boy sheep and girl sheep.

And she wasn't too fond of adults, either. As Matthew liked to point out, this meant Monica hated "just about everyone." He'd recently found the "perfect word" to describe her and had practically dragged her to the library to show her the definition in the dictionary:

mis•an•thrope \ mis'ən thrōp' \ n : one who hates mankind.

"From the Greek," Matthew had added, smiling.

Matthew was different. He definitely wasn't one of the sheep. He was also the only person as smart as she was. Probably smarter, she thought. And he seemed indifferent to the changes going on in his body or anyone else's.

———

Sitting at her desk with her palm cupped under her chin, Monica watched Matthew as he sat, or more precisely, slumped, his head on his desk, dozing through math class. Their teacher, Mr. Brock, busily scratched some equations on the blackboard.

"Who can solve this equation for X? ... Anyone? ... No one? ..." None of the students moved a muscle. Mr. Brock shook his head in disgust. "You're all here to learn, you know. I know all this stuff already. That's why I'm the teacher, get it? Anyone ... oh forget it. Let's ask Matthew, shall we? Matthew? ... Matthew? ... "

The kid at the desk next to Matthew gave him a poke. Matthew raised his head, dazed.

"Huh?" Matthew said, groggily.

"Enjoying your rest, Matthew?" Mr. Brock asked, his voice laced with sarcasm.

"I was ... I was just thinking."

"Uh huh. I wouldn't want to disturb your beauty sleep." The class chuckled.

"That's okay," said Matthew, as if accepting this apology seriously. Monica couldn't help but giggle.

"While you're up, though," said Mr. Brock, "would you mind solving this equation for X?"

Matthew thought for less than a second. "X equals Y squared plus two Y."

"There you go, people," Mr. Brock said. "He learns more while he's asleep than the rest of you do while you're awake." Mr. Brock sat down at his desk at the front of the class. "Thank you, Matt. You can go back to sleep now. In fact, why don't you all go to sleep? Maybe you'll learn something."

After math class, Matthew and Monica sat together on their usual bench for lunch. Matthew peeled back the top of his sandwich to examine the contents.

"It's green, I think, but is it olive green or forest green?" he asked. Monica scrunched her face.

"What *is* that?" she asked in mock horror.

"I don't really know. Mrs. Vines has been watching the Food Network again."

"Looks like some sort of bodily secretion," Monica said. Matthew nodded glumly and took a bite.

"Hmmm, chunky, yet gelatinous. I think it's monkey-brain salad." He licked his lips with feigned enthusiasm. "You want half?"

"Sure," she said and began to eat. Monica almost never had a lunch of her own.

"Your father spent your lunch money again?"

"You know him and his wine cellar. June was a very good month for jug wine," she said. Matthew said nothing.

"You sure are zoning out through a lot of classes these days," she said, changing the subject. Matthew seemed suddenly nervous.

"I've been having a little trouble sleeping, that's all."

"Insomnia?"

"Yeah, I guess."

"Is it nightmares or something?"

"No," Matthew said sharply. Monica saw fear flash through his eyes, just for a moment, then disappear. "Why do you ask?" he said.

"No reason. Just wondering." She knew she'd hit a nerve but decided not to pursue it. They sat in silence for a while, finishing their sandwiches. "So when should I come over tonight?" Monica asked at last.

"Tonight?"

"Telescope night. You were going to show me the Crab Nebula. Don't you remember?"

"Sure ... " Matthew stammered. He hadn't forgotten, but then the prettiest girl in science class had asked if *she* could look through his telescope, and he couldn't say no to *her*, could he? "It's just that tonight probably isn't a good night for it. Mrs. Vines wanted me to help her with some stuff." The lie practically caught in Matthew's throat. "If it's okay with you, I think we'll have to do it another night."

"Sure, another night," Monica said cheerfully. "I'm really looking forward to it, though. I've never seen a galaxy or a nebula, except in photographs, of course. It's so exciting to think the light you see has been traveling for millions of years, just to hit your eye at the exact moment you look through the lens. It's almost like a time machine!"

"Another night. Okay?" Matthew was beginning to feel more than a little guilty.

"Promise?"

"I promise."

That night, with his telescope clock drive tracking the Crab Nebula as it slowly arced across the sky, but with no pretty girl in sight, Matthew realized she wasn't coming. He became suddenly aware of the crickets chirping all around him in the darkness. He had lied to one girl and been stood up by another. He felt rather pathetic.

"She's a no-show, huh?" a voice said, startling him. Monica emerged from behind some bushes.

"What are *you* doing here?" Matthew said. Monica walked over to the telescope and peered in.

"Blondes are so fickle, aren't they?" she said with a smirk as she adjusted the eyepiece. "Maybe your telescope isn't big enough."

"How do you know—"

"One of the girls at school told me about your 'date' tonight."

"Oh."

24

"She was just trying to make a fool of you, you know. They all had a good laugh about it."

Matthew did feel like a fool. And he didn't like Monica rubbing it in. "You shouldn't spy on people," he said.

"I can't help it. I guess it's just scientific curiosity," Monica said, smiling. Then her smile faded. "*You* shouldn't lie to people."

"I'm sorry," Matthew said. He sighed. "I just thought you might be hurt."

"Why should I be hurt? I'm not your girlfriend. I don't care what you do. She's really not your type, though."

"How do you know who's my type?"

"I don't know. I just know she's not your type."

"She is too my type! She's perfectly my type!"

"Why? Because she's beautiful?"

"What's wrong with that?"

"You men are all the same," Monica said. "Always thinking with your dicks." Matthew's jaw clenched.

"At least she looks like a girl," Matthew said. "Not like some people I know."

He regretted it the instant he said it, but it was too late. He watched Monica's expression harden. They stood without speaking for what seemed like a long time. The crickets droned.

"Not everyone gets to be beautiful," she said at last. In a flash, she was on her bike, pedaling away furiously.

"Monica, wait!" he shouted. "I didn't mean, I mean ... " But she was gone.

The crickets seemed louder than ever.

The next day, Monica was not in school. Matthew found lunch lonely without her, classes even more boring than usual. When his last one was finally over, he headed for Monica's.

Matthew rarely went to Monica's house. For one thing, she seemed to spend as little time as possible there herself. The truth was, it wasn't a pleasant place. Sometimes he thought she was ashamed to have anyone, even him, see where she lived.

And then there was her father. "You'll have to excuse him. He leaves a little something to be desired," she'd often say, with a grim half-smile. Her father drank a lot, smoked a lot, and seemed to do little else, judging from the profusion of empty bottles, cans, and ashtrays (always full), and the fact that the house needed painting, the lawn needed mowing, and just about everything else needed cleaning, or maybe just burning.

Matthew walked up the front steps and knocked on the door. There was no answer. He knocked again.

"Anybody home?" He heard footsteps inside, and the door opened.

"What?" Monica asked, expressionless.

"Hi," Matthew said, hoping for any reaction at all, even a frown.

"What do you want?" she asked.

"I just thought I'd drop by and say hello." He tried to act nonchalant. "You weren't in school today. Are you sick?"

"Nope. Anything else?"

"Not really. I just—"

"Okay then. See ya," she said, trying to close the door. Matthew blocked it with his foot.

"Monica, wait!"

"What do you *want*?"

"Can I come in? Please?"

Monica said nothing, let go of the door, and headed back into the house. After a moment's hesitation, Matthew accepted this as an invitation, and walked in.

The house was as messy as ever. It smelled of cigarettes and beer. And it was dark; all the curtains were drawn. In the living room, the

TV was on without the sound, casting a blue glow. He walked past it to the kitchen.

Monica sat at the kitchen table, drinking a Budweiser. Dirty dishes overflowed from the sink onto the counter. The floor was sticky under his sneakers. He sat quietly across the table from her, hoping she would say something. She didn't.

"Your father lets you drink?" he asked, finally breaking the silence.

"My father doesn't 'let' me do anything," she said sharply. "I don't see him around here anywhere. Do you?"

"How long has he been gone this time?"

"Since the day before yesterday."

"What are you going to do? Aren't you worried?"

"No," Monica said, taking a swig. "He'll come back. He always does. I always hope he'll never come back, but he always does."

Matthew didn't know what to say.

"Hey, it's not so bad. At least he doesn't hit me." She swirled her beer around the bottom of the bottle. "Yup, no tyranny here. More like an abdication."

"I'm sorry about last night, Monica. It's just that—"

"Apology accepted," Monica said.

"But I want to explain—"

"I *said* apology accepted. So shut up."

Matthew nodded and shrugged. "At least you *have* a father," he said.

That night at dinner Matthew spent his time pushing his food around his plate, as he'd done for as long as Mrs. Vines could remember.

"Mrs. Vines?"

"Yes, dear?"

"Did you love my dad?"

"Your father was a wonderful man. I loved him very much."

"Do you miss him?"

"Yes."

"Do you ever dream about him?"

"Sometimes."

"Good dreams?"

"Of course, dear."

"Do you think he could still be alive?"

Tears glistened in her eyes. "Oh, I know it's hard, but he's gone from us to a better place. Someday, when our time comes, we'll all be together again. And your mother, too."

For the rest of their dinner, they were silent.

6.

Wind whips across the cliffs. Lightning stings the darkness with blinding flashes, coming furiously now, like a drunken, syncopated strobe. We cling desperately to the sheer rock face, our feet scrambling for footing. The thunder seems to shake the earth. Above us, we see an entrance to a cave...

... and we are in a dim, torch-lit passage. We hear chanting ahead of us. We follow the sound into a huge chamber, whose dimensions we can barely see—the darkness sucking up the firelight—but we know its immensity from the echoes.

The medicine men are chanting. They stand in a circle around an altar. We approach. One of them stares at us, his eyes wide, deep, terrifying... He hands us a knife.

"The tribe depends on you now," he says. "You are the One." We feel the knife in our hands, see the flash of firelight reflected in the blade. A man lies before us, on the altar, wrapped in blankets. He seems weak and frail. We raise the knife to strike the blow!

Suddenly, his face turns to us, and we recognize him. "Help me. Please help me ... son!"

Matthew jerked up out of a deep sleep, drenched in sweat, his heart pounding. The same dream again. He sat for a while, felt his heartbeat slow, then dressed quickly and snuck out into the night. The cool night air and the moonlight calmed him; a breeze dried the sweat on his forehead. He walked quickly until he reached Monica's house.

He stood outside for a few minutes, afraid to ring the doorbell so late and not sure what else to do. At last, he grabbed a handful of gravel from the driveway and stood below her bedroom window. He tossed a pebble against the glass. It made a sharp click. He waited a moment, then tossed another. A light came on in her bedroom, and the window opened. Monica peered out.

"Who is it?" Monica whispered.

"Me."

"Matthew?"

"Yeah."

"What are you doing here?"

"I'm sorry. Did I wake you?"

"What kind of stupid question is that?"

They sat together in her backyard, side by side on rusty old swings that squeaked and creaked with every movement.

"Is this thing safe?" Matthew asked.

"Probably not. So how long have you been having these dreams?"

"A while, I guess. But more lately."

"That explains your recent—what's that disease where you fall asleep?"

"Narcolepsy," Matthew said.

"Right."

"Anyway, at first I couldn't remember much. But lately I'm remembering more. The dream is always the same—the same place, the same people. It seems so real."

"What kind of place?"

"I don't know. A cave, I think. But huge, like a cathedral."

Monica listened intently, seriously. Matthew began to relax.

"You think it's a real place?"

"I don't know. But I'm sure the people in the dream are Hopi."

"Hopi Indians?"

"Right. They're in Arizona. My dad was very interested in the Hopi and their prophecies."

"Then it makes sense that you might dream about them, doesn't it?"

"Yes, but ... "

"But what?"

"I don't know. In the dream, my father's sick, I think. He wants me to help him. At least at first. And then ... " His voice trailed off.

"And then what? What else happens in the dream?"

Matthew closed his eyes, thinking. He could see the altar and the knife in his hand. But he was afraid to tell her.

"Nothing, I mean, it's not clear. The dream ends, that's all."

He suddenly noticed that Monica was in her pajamas. "Are you cold?" he asked.

"No, I'm fine."

"I'm sorry about this, I mean, about waking you up in the middle of the night. I just needed someone to talk to, and I can't talk to Mrs. Vines. Not about this, anyway. She'd just get worried and send me to a doctor or something."

Monica looked thoughtful.

"I guess you still miss him," she said. Matthew nodded. "They're just dreams, Matt. That's all. Just dreams."

"Right," Matthew said softly.

Later, when he got back from Monica's, the house was dark and quiet. Mrs. Vines was still asleep. He didn't go back to his room but instead went straight to his father's study.

In the years since his father's disappearance, Matthew had often wondered about his father's last expedition. Where had he been going? Why had it been so secret? Over time, the urgency of these questions had faded, but with the dreams becoming more vivid and more frequent, now he wanted answers.

He turned on the light over his father's desk. Matthew had always loved the room, and he and Mrs. Vines had both resolved not to change it. Whenever he entered it, he was flooded with memories, and this time was no exception. He felt his father's presence and shivered.

Most of the wall space was used for bookshelves, stuffed to overflowing with books on a variety of subjects; over the years, Matthew had looked through most of them. On the desk were a few piles of papers under geode paperweights, and some framed photographs. One was a picture of his mother. She had died when he was born, and he did not remember her. In the picture she had a faint smile and kind eyes, and Matthew thought she was beautiful. He knew his father must have missed her terribly.

Next to that was a picture of his father and himself. They were smiling and happy in the photo, and Matthew felt his throat tighten.

Finally, there was a picture of his father standing next to a white-haired old man. The photo was signed, "To Jonathan Wilkes, former student, but friend always. Theodore Schnabel." Matthew knew Schnabel had been his father's professor at the university and was the author of a number of the books on his father's shelf. The professor had come to the house a few times, even once or twice after his father's disappearance, but it had been years since Matthew had seen him.

He sat back in his father's chair, his eyes staring deep into those of the old professor, and suddenly he knew what he had to do. He was sure the dreams would not just go away, and, though he didn't know why, he had a feeling the professor could help.

Between classes at school the next day, Matthew called the university, only to discover that Professor Schnabel was on sabbatical. A call to the professor's home number just rang and rang. He'd have to visit him in person.

During lunch, Monica asked Matthew why he seemed so preoccupied, but he decided not to tell her. Matthew's last class seemed like it would never end, band practice after school was way too long, and dinner—for which he was a good twenty minutes late—dragged on forever, with Mrs. Vines in the mood to hear about even the most trivial details of his day.

Finally, when dinner was over and he'd cleared the table, Matthew made a quick excuse to Mrs. Vines and was off on his bike into the twilight.

7.

Professor Schnabel's large old Victorian house sat on a little hill at the end of the street, nestled behind oak trees shrouding it in darkness. It was somehow eerie, and as Matthew approached it on his bike, his palms got sweaty. He thought for a moment he might come back when it was light, but the fear of another dream-filled night stiffened his resolve. He left his bike on the front path, walked to the front door, and knocked. After a moment, the door opened, and a middle-aged woman stood in the doorway, glaring.

"Yes?"

Matthew gulped. "I'd like to see Professor Schnabel, please."

"The professor cannot see anyone."

"I just wanted to talk to him for a second."

"That would not be possible."

"Is he away?"

"The professor is not receiving any visitors at this time." She closed the door.

Matthew didn't know what to do. He couldn't just give up. He needed to see Schnabel. He was about to knock again when it occurred to him to try the doorknob. Unlocked. He quietly, very quietly, opened the door and walked in.

He found himself in a front hallway. The first thing he noticed was the smell. It smelled old. And in fact, everything looked old, too. Old rugs, old wallpaper, old furniture—even the telephone had a dial instead of buttons. This house hasn't changed in fifty years, he thought. He felt like he was in an old movie.

The woman who had answered the door was nowhere to be seen, but there was a light coming from the kitchen, at the end of the hall. To either side were French doors with glass panes, leading into rooms that were almost completely dark. He chose the door on the right and walked in.

Matthew wished he had a flashlight. But there was enough light coming from the hallway and moonlight from outside to see he was in a living room. He'd decided to turn on a lamp when he stopped dead. Faintly, very faintly, he could hear music coming from the back of the house. He tiptoed across the living room to the only other door, opened it, and walked through.

The new room was darker, and he felt for a light switch on the wall. Turning it on, he almost screamed. A giant creature loomed over him, its huge, angry eyes staring at him. He jumped away, bumping into a table, and heard glass shatter on the floor. He knew the beast was about to pounce.

But the thing didn't move. It had great wings and many sets of eyes, but as the adrenaline rush faded, Matthew saw it was not living. It was a totem pole, carved from wood, with many faces and symbols stacked one on top of the other. Matthew knew it was made by a tribe of the Pacific Northwest; the faces and symbols represented a family history. It still seemed a little menacing, but beautiful, too. Next to the totem pole was a life-size, carved figure of an Indian brave, a "wooden Indian" of the kind used in the old days to advertise cigars. Matthew sensed the irony of the two standing next to each other, and his racing heart began to slow.

He looked around. It was an incredible collection of Native-American artifacts, the larger ones freestanding, many others in display cases or mounted on the walls. Farther in were more cases full of books. He examined the titles. Most of them related to Native American history and culture. A museum, Matthew thought. The professor's own private museum. He felt he could spend years in this room, happily absorbing all it could teach him.

And the music was louder now; Matthew could hear it clearly. Beethoven. But it was coming from outside the house, and Matthew looked through a window into the backyard. Through the darkness he could see a large shed; the music was coming from there. A light flickered as if there were a fire inside.

Just then he heard footsteps behind him. "What are you doing?" the woman barked.

Matthew whirled. "I'm sorry," he stammered. "I just wanted to see—"

"Get out, young man. You have no business being here. If you don't leave this instant, I'll call the police!"

"Yes, ma'am." Matthew scurried past her toward the front door. In moments, he was out on the front porch.

"You have no right to violate the professor's privacy. I don't want to see you here again." She closed the door, and this time, he heard her lock it.

This is really weird, he thought. *What's the big mystery?* He remembered the movie, *The Fly,* and he imagined the professor, a mutated half-man, half-fly, hiding in the basement, unable to see anyone, struggling desperately for a cure…

He snapped out of his daydream and headed down the path to his bicycle. A quick look over his shoulder revealed the woman peering at him through the curtains. He got on his bike and pretended to ride away but stopped as soon as he was out of sight behind some hedges. He left his bike and walked toward the back of the house. Sneaking toward the shed on foot, he could hear the music again. The Ninth Symphony. There was no way to peek inside, so he chose the direct approach. He knocked.

At first there was no answer, so he knocked again. "What's all that banging!" a voice yelled from within. "Can't we have some peace and quiet around here?!"

"Professor?" Matthew said in a loud whisper. "Professor?" He knocked again.

He could hear shuffling footsteps. Then a metallic crash followed by a loud thump. "What do you want?" asked the voice from behind the door.

"Are you Professor Schnabel?"

"Might be. Who wants to know?"

The door suddenly opened a crack. An old man with round spectacles peered out. The professor scrunched his face and stroked his chin. "You seem a little young to be one of my students. Though I suppose everyone looks young to me these days. Who are you?"

"My name is Matthew Wilkes. You knew my father, Jonathan Wilkes. He was a—"

The professor slammed the door in Matthew's face.

Matthew was dumbfounded. *This is crazy,* he thought. He knocked again. "Professor?"

"Go away!" the professor bellowed from behind the door.

"I need to talk to you about my father, Professor! Please!" The door opened a little wider this time, and the professor's head poked out like a turtle's from its shell.

"The last thing I want in my life is another Wilkes! Jonathan Wilkes is quite enough for one lifetime, thank you. Now goodbye!" He slammed the door again.

Matthew was about to knock for a third time when once again it occurred to him to try the doorknob. It turned, and he opened the door, trying to think of something to say.

But what he saw, filling the room from floor to ceiling, left him speechless. There were flashing lights, and electric sparks jumping between long, insect-like antennae. Glowing vacuum tubes and old CRT television screens. Wires and tubes branching like a forest of glass and plastic trees, and a blur of digits in a sea of liquid-crystal displays. Intermittent patterns of light slinked through the apparatus like the coils of a snake, sometimes slowly, sometimes rapidly, seeming to dance to the Beethoven playing on an old stereo in the corner of the workshop. Matthew saw figure eights, crystalline shapes, animal shapes, and floral patterns, all coalescing and then dissolving before his eyes, as if unconnected to the apparatus that produced them, swirling within it like ghosts in the machine. He was mesmerized by the patterns, straining to see them; it was like looking for shapes in clouds, as he and his father had done years before, lying on their backs on grassy hills, staring up at the sky. Or like trying to trace the outlines of the constellations in a seemingly random field of stars. It was a feeling like daydreaming—a warm trance Matthew wanted to last forever.

"It's beautiful!" Matthew didn't even realize he'd said it aloud.

The professor, who'd been busy tinkering with the strange device, stopped his work at the sound of Matthew's voice.

"It *is* rather magnificent," Schnabel said with pride, calmly taking in his own creation. It seemed to have the same effect on him it had on Matthew, and for a strange moment they stood silently side by side, awed.

"What is it?" Matthew said finally, waving his arms to indicate the whole incomprehensible roomful.

"What is it, you ask? Yes, what is it? That's what *I* would like to know," the professor said.

"You mean you don't know what it is?"

"No, no. Of course I don't know!"

"Didn't you build it?"

"Oh my yes, and quite an effort, I can tell you."

"But if you don't know what it is, how did you know how to build it?"

"He shows me, and suddenly it's all very clear," the professor said.

"Someone shows you?" Matthew asked.

"Yes, yes," the professor said. "How else would I know? He shows me, and I build what I see." The professor, who had been carefully scrutinizing one small screw, now began adjusting it with a screwdriver. "I do hope it's finished soon," he said with a sigh.

"Who shows you?"

"Hmmm?" asked the professor, ignoring Matthew. He was totally absorbed in the machine now, turning a series of screws—one, then another, then another.

"Professor!" said Matthew, almost shouting. "Who? Who shows you what to do?"

"Why, your father of course," the old man said.

"My father?" Matthew's mind raced.

"Yes, yes. In some sort of danger, I'm sure. Just like Jonathan to go and get himself into a jam. And now ... " He suddenly occupied himself with tightening a stubborn screw. "And now I've got to bail him out. Jonathan and his crazy ideas ... There. That did it," he said triumphantly, winning his battle with the screw. He turned his attention back to Matthew.

"I knew it would happen, you see," the old man continued. "I told him. But, of course, he never listened to me." He peered back at his device. "No, no, that's not right," he said, shaking his head.

Matthew was getting steadily more confused. "Have you *seen* my father?" he asked.

"Of course."

"You've seen him? Then he's alive!" Matthew's heart was pounding.

"Alive?" the professor said. He looked thoughtful, as if considering the question for the first time. "Well now, I really wouldn't know if he's alive or not, but if you want my opinion, I think he's a ghost, and as we all know, you have to be dead to be a ghost."

Another turn of the screwdriver, and sparks began to fly in all directions. The professor's spectacles sparkled from the reflections. "Now we're getting somewhere," he said, admiring the fireworks.

"A ghost? What do you mean, a ghost? When do you see him?" Matthew asked, raising his voice over the crackling. The professor ignored him. He grabbed the old man's shoulder. "Professor!"

"Please, I'm busy!"

"Professor!" Matthew shouted again, shaking Schnabel vigorously. "When do you see my father?"

The sparks stopped abruptly, and the professor sighed.

"In the dreams. I thought you understood all this."

Matthew shook his head, trying to clear it. *He has dreams, too!*

"In the dreams, my father tells you to build ... this?" Matthew asked, gesturing to the huge apparatus.

"Yes, yes!"

"How do you know he's dead, Professor?"

"I don't know how I know. In fact, I don't know at all. I don't know whether he's alive or dead, in heaven or in hell. Who knows? I don't."

"Maybe he's not dead, Professor! Maybe he *is* alive!"

The professor mused for a moment. "I suppose it's possible he's alive," he said. "Who can say? I thought it was all nonsense, you see. But I suppose he did find something out there after all."

Matthew had the feeling of almost remembering something, like having a word on the tip of your tongue you can't quite get out. Everything—the dreams, the huge contraption—it was all connected, he knew. And he was sure his father was alive. But where? And what had happened?

"What was my father searching for, Professor?"

"The source of the legend, of course. Must I explain everything to you?"

40

"What legend?"

"The legend! The prophecy! Your father believed it was all true. I thought it was all poppycock, of course. But I suppose he was right. He usually was, you know. As if it matters now. Always getting himself into trouble, that one..." His voice trailed off into memories of the past.

"This legend, is it a Hopi legend?"

"Indeed!"

Matthew was so surprised to finally get a straight answer that for a moment he didn't know what to say. His father had disappeared in Arizona, where the Hopi Mesas were. And the Hopi were in his dreams. It all made some sort of sense. Sort of.

Suddenly the old professor shook his head and wagged his finger at Matthew. "I see that look in your eyes, like your father," the old man said. "You want to go searching for him, don't you?"

"Yes."

The old man sighed. "Well, I suppose it can't be helped. Like father, like son, I suppose." The two of them stood quietly for a moment, and the professor smiled kindly at Matthew. "Take care of yourself, my boy," the old man said.

"I will." Matthew thought he saw tears in the corners of the professor's eyes.

At the doorway, Matthew looked back for a moment, but the old man was already back in another world.

8.

It was dark when Matthew left the professor's house, and he pedaled furiously through the night, gliding through the silent streets. He felt like he was flying.

He's alive! I know he's alive! He chanted it to himself like a mantra.

He could not tell Mrs. Vines, of course. In fact, no one would really believe him, he knew. No one except Monica.

Monica's house was dark when he arrived, but the front door was ajar.

"Monica?" he said, entering cautiously. He found Monica in the kitchen, wiping her eyes. "The front door was open," he said.

"My father must have left it open on his way out."

"He was here tonight?"

"Oh yes. He and I spent some quality time."

"What happened to you? You have a black eye!"

"I slipped in the tub."

"Ouch!" Matthew winced. "Are you okay?"

"Fine. It looks worse than it is. What are you doing here, anyway?"

"It's about my father!" Matthew said, excitement bursting out of him. "What about him?"

Matthew pulled up a chair and sat down. "I went to see a friend of his, this old professor, and you won't believe it, but he's been having dreams, too! About my father! And he's building something, some sort of strange device. It's like one of those old science fiction movies. He says my father is telling him how to build it, in the dreams. I don't really understand it all … but I know he's alive, I just know it, and he needs my help!"

Monica was just shaking her head. "I can't believe you. I really can't. When are you going to get over this obsession with your father? He's dead! Can't you accept that?"

Matthew felt like he had been slapped in the face. "Didn't you hear anything I said?"

"I heard it," Monica said. It was as if all her feelings about her own father, about all fathers, about the very concept of father, were boiling over. "I heard it," she repeated. "It sounds pretty crazy to me. If you'd stop to think about it for a second, you'd realize it, too."

"You don't understand," Matthew said, pleading with her. "If the professor is having dreams, too, then they can't be just dreams. It would be too much of a coincidence, don't you see?"

"All I see is someone who believes something because he *wants* to believe it. Because he believes that somehow his father is going to solve all his problems, to make everything right with the world. Well, I can tell you it's not true. Someday you'll realize you don't need your father, or anybody else. The only person you need is yourself."

Her voice was thick with anger. Matthew looked into her eyes and realized she'd been crying. "Your father gave you that black eye, didn't he?" he said softly.

"Why don't you just leave? Go look for your stupid father."

Matthew stood for a moment in stunned silence. "My father is not your father," he said finally.

"All fathers are the same."

"Fine, I'll see you later," he said, storming out.

Monica watched him go, heard the front door slam, and almost ran after him. Instead, she slumped against the door and cried.

That night, after Mrs. Vines was asleep, Matthew prepared for his journey. He packed a small bag with some clothes, remembering at the last minute to pack underwear and a toothbrush. He raided the piggy bank his father had given him when he was four; it yielded a little more than fifty dollars. Combined with a few weeks' allowance, and after a raid on Mrs. Vines's grocery stash, his expedition was still starting with a budget of less than a hundred dollars.

Long after midnight, he went to his father's study. He found an old map of the Southwest and traced the route he'd take to Arizona and the Hopi mesas. And he took a book from his father's shelf, a book of Hopi prophecies. As he sat for a few minutes at his father's desk, doubts crept into his mind...

This is crazy. Maybe I shouldn't go. Maybe I do need a psychiatrist. Maybe—

No! You're just getting cold feet, that's all—

Or maybe Monica was right. You just think he's alive because that's what you want to believe—

But what about the dreams?

They're just dreams. Besides, even if he were alive, how are you going to find him? You can't just wander around the desert alone.

Matthew suddenly realized he was having more than just cold feet. He was scared. But not scared of being lost and alone, not scared of being wrong about his father and finding nothing. No, he was afraid of being right, afraid of what he might find, afraid of whatever it was his father had found.

He wrote a note to Mrs. Vines and stuck it on the refrigerator:

Left early for school. Staying at Brian's house this weekend.
Love, Matt

He hated to lie to her, but he needed a few days' head start, and he knew when she finally discovered the truth, she'd call the police. He told himself he'd call her in a few days and tell her not to worry.

It was dark when he got his bike out of the garage; sunrise was still half an hour away. He was about to ride off when he noticed someone with a bicycle waiting for him at the end of the driveway, under the lone street lamp: it was Monica.

"Leaving so soon?" she said. "You don't waste any time."

"Yeah."

"I wanted to tell you I'm really sorry," she said quietly. "I guess I was angry at my dad, and I took it out on you. I know how important this is to you, and I know you're probably scared. You need support from a friend, not doubt. I'm sorry."

Matthew felt for a second as if he might cry. "It's okay," he said.

"Anyway, I'm all packed and ready to go," Monica said, suddenly cheerful.

"Go?"

"I'm not going to let you do this alone."

"But—"

"Don't argue. I want to come with you."

"Are you sure?"

"Yep!"

"But what are you going to tell your fath—never mind."

"Let's go," she said, and they pedaled off into the darkness.

9.

The workshop was a whirl of activity, humming and sparking, glowing and flashing, alive with the monstrosity the professor knew, just *knew*, was on the verge of . . .

Of what?

Professor Schnabel didn't know what. But in the last few days his activity had reached a fever pitch. If he'd been able to stop and think, he would have realized it had been over a week since he'd slept, even longer since he'd eaten. The work was completely consuming him.

Almost there! Almost finished! he thought, scurrying excitedly around the huge device. On the stereo, Beethoven's great Ninth Symphony was reaching its spectacular climax.

Only the central part of the thing was dark now. He knew that when the center came alive, it would be done. How did he know that? He didn't know . . .

A remote part of his mind considered the purpose of the machine. *Is it a nuclear reactor? That would explain the plutonium. Hmm . . . I do hope it's not a bomb . . .*

No. He was sending a message, he somehow knew. An important message, a message from a long time ago. A message that *must be sent!* His thoughts spiraled faster and faster. *The message* must *be sent because it has already been received!* he thought gleefully. *Try to figure that one out!* His exhausted brain was reeling, his mind and body both completely spent.

Now he stood in front of a row of computer screens. Trace lines ran across each screen slowly, beeping like heartbeats on EKGs. The beeps were out of phase at first, coming in a staggered pattern. His attention darted from one screen to another, then to the apparatus, where waves of light and sparks began to cascade through the machine so it seemed somehow to be spinning, though it was, in fact, completely stationary. The various frequencies began to synchronize, as if the many heartbeats were becoming one.

Almost there! Almost done!

He approached the huge main switch of the device, a three-foot-long lever that would close the main power contacts. He stood, arm raised, holding the lever, ready to slam it home, his eyes blazing in the flashing, strobing lights. He paused, savoring the last moment before the plunge, then threw the switch closed.

The last thing I'll ever do . . .

From the core of the machine, the central crystalline sphere began to glow, brighter and brighter. And from the depths of the machine, as if from the depths of the earth, a great hum emerged, like a chorus of Tibetan monks, a cosmic "Ohmmmmm," the sound of the infinite.

And the professor knew he had succeeded.

Night still possessed the town, and the professor's workshop was a small pool of light, an oasis in a desert of darkness. As the last chords of the Beethoven died away, the old professor's laughter seemed to echo for miles and miles.

10.

It was just a big tank of water. That was the key to the experiment, a big tank of water, and all you did was watch it. Constantly. Twenty-four hours a day. Seven days a week. Fifty-two weeks a year . . .

Not the most exciting experiment. Kind of like watching grass grow.

The water was in complete darkness, far underground. In theory, therefore, it was shielded from almost every kind of electromagnetic wave or particle, except for the one the experimenters were looking for. And, every once in a while, out of the trillions upon trillions upon trillions of water molecules in the tank, a single molecule would just happen to be struck by one of those mysterious particles that most of the time were passing through the tank, and through the entire earth for that matter, effortlessly, at the speed of light, minding their own business: neutrinos.

Struck by a neutrino, the water molecule would emit a flash. Like a flashbulb. Only dimmer. Much, much dimmer. So the experimenters were looking for a small flash of light in a big tank of water. A small flash. Very, very small. Not work for the naked eye, of course. The tank was surrounded by highly sensitive detectors, which were connected to computers. And, after waiting a while, what came out of the computers was the signature of the neutrino.

On that particular day in Australia, Down Under as they say, on a winter's day in July (the seasons, of course, being reversed on that side of the globe), one of the experimenters had just sat down for a cup of tea and a Vegemite sandwich when, though this dramatic event would still have been as invisible to the naked eye as striking a match a thousand miles away, the whole tank lit up.

If the computers had actually gone up in smoke, dramatic sparks, and explosions, the experimenter would not, in fact, have been any more surprised than he actually was. Mid-bite, he sat staring at the computer screen for what would have seemed like a very long time to anyone who might have been watching him (no one was), entranced, while the Vegemite grew sticky and began to cling to the roof of his mouth.

The next few hours were frenzied; checks and double checks confirmed there had been no glitches, no malfunctions, no human error. The phenomenon had, in fact, occurred, despite its impossibility. A series of emails followed alerting the experiment team to the event, beginning the search for an explanation for the unexplainable.

Any such explanation was likely to be found in the stars—a supernova, a stellar collapse, perhaps a large-scale solar event—and so there was more emailing and Skyping to observatories and satellite ground stations around the world, probing for information without tipping their own discovery. In the back of their minds, the team thought Nobel Prize, and it wouldn't have been the first time a great discovery was made by accident. They had certainly discovered something; now they needed an explanation, and until they had one, they would play their cards close to the chest.

But halfway around the world, in a small computer room in Langley, Virginia, in the headquarters of the Central Intelligence Agency, someone guessed their hand.

11.

Arnold Robinson sat in the dark office, watching smoke curl around his boss's ears. That the office was dark was to be expected; his boss, Jack Walker, seemed to prefer dark places. That preference, combined with Walker's distinctly nocturnal habits (if he slept, it had to be during the day, Robinson thought, as Walker was always up all night, and rumor had it he didn't sleep at all), made Walker the butt of many a vampire joke. Behind his back, of course. *Never* to his face.

That Walker was smoking was also to be expected; Robinson never saw Walker without a cigarette. Why, though, did Walker insist on wearing dark glasses? With the room as dark as it was, Robinson wondered how Walker could see anything at all. And when you added Walker's shoulder-length hair, Robinson thought he looked less like a spy and more like a rock star. All in all, a most peculiar man to work for.

Jack Walker was, however, the best in the business, and Robinson, who'd been handpicked to work as his assistant, felt justifiably proud. Robinson had a multitude of talents: he was athletic (a former track star), spoke five languages fluently, and was a brilliant scientist and mathematician. He'd had numerous career options, and the main reason he hadn't chosen to do research at MIT, or to make millions at Google, was his taste for the exotic and the unexplained, like the mysterious Mr. Walker. And so, though he knew himself to be a good and decent young man, Robinson was also a spy for the CIA, and he sat there in the dark office across from a man who, shrouded in smoke, looked rather like Mephistopheles.

"Can you speculate as to what they might have discovered?" Walker asked.

"They were looking for neutrinos. I would guess they found some."

One of the tasks Walker had assigned to Robinson was keeping a close watch on the global scientific community. He monitored the Internet, intercepted e-mail, hacked into computers, even used simple wiretaps. Some of it was legal; some of it wasn't.

"Their main contacts," Robinson continued, "have been with observatories. They're looking for some sort of astronomical event, presumably to account for whatever it is they observed."

"Do we know when they observed whatever it is they observed?"

"Hard to say. They're scouring for data in a window between July twenty-first and twenty-third."

"Have you tried hacking their computer system?"

"Yes. No luck."

Walker sat impassively, smoking and thinking. "Why do I think this is important?"

"Do you want me to guess?" Robinson asked.

"Hmmm, not really. I think you should make some travel arrangements, Mr. Robinson."

"Travel arrangements?"

Walker just cocked his head and smiled. "Why do I think this is important?" he said again, and this time Robinson said nothing.

12.

Matthew stared out the window of the bus, watching the telephone lines, which seemed to weave up and down as they streaked past, like giant guitar strings vibrating in slow motion. Monica, who'd gotten a cherry Slushie at their last rest stop, sat next to him, happily slurping away.

"Ow!"

"What's wrong?" Matthew asked.

"Brain freeze!" she managed to say between winces.

"I hate it when that happens," he said, forcing a smile.

"Are you okay?" Monica asked.

"I'm fine. I'm just thinking."

Monica got out Matthew's map and unfolded it. "Boy, no one uses these now! Anyway, the way I figure it, we'll catch the bus from Santa Fe to Gallup and spend the night there. Then it's west to the Hopi mesas."

"What if there's no bus there?"

"We'll hitchhike."

"Hitchhike? I don't know…"

"Scared?" Monica smirked.

"No. It's just that, I mean—"

"Scared." Monica said, nodding. "Some Indiana Jones you'll make."

"Speaking of which, can I take this off now?" he asked, tugging on the brim of the hat she'd brought along for him.

"But it's so perfect! Right out of *Raiders of the Lost Ark*. You look great."

Matthew sighed.

"By the way," Monica said, "what did you tell Mrs. Vines?"

"I left her a note. I told her I was staying at Brian Robbins's house for the weekend."

"Brian Robbins hates you."

"This is true. But she doesn't know that. She only has the faintest inkling of the true scope of my unpopularity."

Monica smiled.

"It'll give us some time, anyway," he continued. "I couldn't have her calling the police before we had a couple of days' head start."

"She'll worry."

"I'll call her."

"She'll still worry."

"Yeah. It can't be helped. She couldn't possibly have understood."

"I wish I did," she said as her gaze drifted out the window, where, for the first time on their trip, there was desert.

13.

Robinson had never been to Australia. The flight was a long one, and he was grateful Walker had him book first class. The seats were comfortable and the food good. His boss, however, was more inscrutable than ever.

For most of the flight, Walker simply sat and stared. He did not sleep; he simply sat. Robinson couldn't tell whether Walker was deep in thought, or whether he'd somehow managed to just turn his brain off. Either way it was disconcerting. Walker's palms were turned upward on his knees, and Robinson recognized the position as a mark of Buddhist training. Walker would have made a good monk, Robinson thought.

It was early morning when they arrived at Sydney Airport. Their diplomatic credentials sped them through customs, and after another much shorter flight on a small propeller plane to Broken Hill, they quickly headed out of town in a rented Range Rover, Robinson behind the wheel. Walker gave curt instructions for their route, without, Robinson noted, consulting the vehicle's GPS. They did not stop to rest, and Robinson was glad he'd slept a little on the plane. It took three more hours to reach the experiment site, an abandoned mine at the edge of the desert; Walker briefed Robinson in the last ten minutes of their drive.

Their visit was remarkably brief. Speaking with a flawless Australian accent, Walker became Professor Jack Bowles, from the University of Sydney, and Robinson became his American graduate assistant. Their meeting with the experimenters—a Professor Taylor and his three young associates—which Walker had arranged himself, was to include a tour of the facility, but Walker delayed the tour by asking for tea and then regaling his increasingly uncertain colleagues with a technical discourse that even Robinson, with his MIT background, could only vaguely follow. Now Robinson excused himself to use the bathroom, snuck into the computer room, accessed the experimenters' main database, broke their access code, and downloaded their data onto a flash drive. Robinson returned from his covert activity to find their hosts sitting slack-jawed, staring with glazed eyes at Walker, who had clearly been talking nonstop during Robinson's absence. On cue, Walker's cell phone conveniently chirped, and one quick, completely fabricated emergency phone call later, Walker canceled their scheduled tour of the neutrino facility, apologized for the sudden change in plans, and declined an offer for lunch. Less than an hour after their arrival, Walker and Robinson were back in the Range Rover, leaving their hosts waving goodbye and looking puzzled.

"What were you talking about back there?" Robinson asked when they were safely away.

"Neutron stars."

"Since when do you know so much about neutron stars?"

"I made it all up," Walker said, without even a hint of a smile. Robinson shook his head in amazement.

Meanwhile, their mission had been a complete success. The event in question had been a multiple neutrino detection on July 23rd at 13:23, ACST. Robinson knew enough physics to marvel at the discovery. It was indeed an unprecedented observation, undoubtedly of tremendous scientific importance, but the reason for Walker's interest in it was still a mystery. And Robinson was becoming more and more curious.

Back on the road, with the Outback stretching around them in all directions, the neutrino complex seemed a distant memory. Soon they would be on a plane, Robinson knew. Walker clearly had no intention of staying even one night. Their entire stay in Australia would be less than twenty-four hours.

Then without warning, Walker told Robinson to veer off onto a dirt road.

"I'm afraid that would take us in the wrong direction," Robinson said.

"You must be hungry, we'll stop to eat," Walker replied. "I know a place…"

Their rest stop was an Aboriginal settlement at the base of some hills. Robinson wondered how Walker knew of its existence; there was no village marked on any map. The settlement was nothing more than a scattering of shacks and a few rickety pickup trucks. As they stopped the Range Rover, several Aborigine men emerged from one of the shacks. Robinson couldn't tell if they recognized Walker, though they didn't seem surprised to have visitors.

A young man dressed in jeans and a T-shirt approached Walker, and they spoke. They did not speak English. After a moment, the young man turned to Robinson.

"Come with me," he said to Robinson, speaking English now with a vaguely Australian accent. "I'll get you something to eat."

What he gave him was some sort of stew; Robinson decided not to ask what was in it. It tasted okay, but Robinson barely noticed. He was preoccupied with Walker, who wasn't eating but instead was off talking with a man Robinson figured must be the tribal shaman. He was an old man, very old with a grizzled beard, and Walker was sitting cross-legged across from him. Robinson could not hear what they were saying, but he could see Walker seemed enthralled, like a young student sitting at his teacher's feet. In a flash Robinson realized this meeting was the true purpose of their stop, not the food. Walker was proving to be stranger and full of more surprises than Robinson could ever have guessed. But his behavior wasn't just strange. Walker seemed to have an agenda he was keeping to himself. And Robinson did not like being kept in the dark.

Walker and the old man talked for what seemed like an hour. Then, abruptly, the meeting was over, and Robinson and Walker were on the road back to town. In the rearview mirror, Robinson watched the old man staring at them, motionless, until the man and then the village became a speck at the foot of the hills.

"Excuse me for asking, but what was that all about?"

"I have a great interest in tribal cultures. A consuming interest. I have found that such cultures often have a sensitivity to things about which modern man remains blissfully unaware."

"Did you ask the old man about neutrinos?"

"How perceptive of you to ask. In fact, I did."

"And?"

"It has nothing to do with them."

"So he didn't know what you were talking about."

"Oh no, I didn't say that," Walker said with a grin. "I didn't say that."

14.

It was long past sunset when the bus dropped Matthew and Monica off at a small outdoor stop under a single street lamp. They watched the bus disappear down the highway, heading out across the desert. The small town was dark and quiet.

"Maybe we should have stayed back in Gallup," Matthew said. "At least that seemed like a city. I mean, they had a McDonald's."

"Since when is McDonald's a sign of civilization?"

They walked slowly down the empty street.

"Seems like the whole town closes for the night," Matthew said.

"There must be somewhere we can stay."

The neon MOTEL sign turned their skin orange as they walked across the courtyard to their cabin.

"He made me nervous," Matthew said about the man who'd rented them the room.

"*Psycho*. Alfred Hitchcock. 1960," Monica said.

"Right. I'm sure the room has a nice shower."

"I think I'll take a bath."

The room was seedy and old.

"Hmm ... " Matthew said, staring at the single bed.

"What do you want for twenty bucks?"

"Hmm ... " Matthew repeated.

"It's not so bad."

"The bed's kind of small. Maybe I should sleep on the floor."

"Don't be silly. What are you afraid of?"

"I'm not afraid," Matthew said.

"Well, I'm not either," Monica said.

"Good."

"Good."

"Right."

"So it's settled. We'll both sleep in the bed."

"Right."

"Right."

Later, Matthew sat reading a book about the Pueblo Indians, by the light of a small lamp on a night table whose single drawer was empty save for its customary bible. He read about the Hopi and their life on the high mesas, now part of the Hopi reservation. He read of kivas, sacred ceremonial chambers, sometimes built underground, centuries ago built in towers by the ancient Anasazi tribes to the north. He read of the Kachina religion, where masked spirits of the dead danced and interceded with the gods. He read of rainmakers, he read of winter people and summer people, squash people and turquoise people, and the disputes between the Hopi and the Navaho nation. And he read of secret societies, ancient in origin, whose private histories wound through hundreds of years of life on the mesas.

The door was open to the bathroom, where Monica was taking a bath.

"It has something to do with secret societies, I think," Matthew said.

"What?" asked Monica from the tub.

"Hopi secret societies. According to this book, some of them still exist." He got up, still reading, and walked toward the bathroom. "Maybe if we ask around the reservation we'll find someone who knows."

"If they really are secret societies, they're not going to tell *you* their secrets, are they?"

59

"I don't know, I—" Matthew stopped mid-sentence and looked up from his book. Monica was in the tub, surrounded by suds, and suddenly he felt very self-conscious. He was staring at her. For a moment they were both silent, then she smiled.

"Oops. Sorry," Matthew said, and he retreated to the bedroom.

Later, they were side by side in the bed, in their pajamas.

"Monica?"

"What?"

"Do you think I'm crazy?"

"Why would I think you were crazy?" she asked.

"I don't know. For believing all this. For believing my dad is alive. For believing my dreams are true. Haven't you thought that maybe I'm just losing my mind, that Professor Schnabel is just an old lunatic? Maybe my dad was nuts, too."

"I've read that insanity can be genetic," she said. "You could have inherited it, I suppose."

They both lay quietly for a while.

"Monica?"

"What?"

"When you did it for the first time, was it what you expected?"

"Did what?"

"You know ... "

"Oh."

"I've never done it before," Matthew said.

"I know."

"Well? Was it what you thought it would be? Was it okay?"

Monica said nothing for a while. "I've never done it either," she said at last.

"You haven't? But Brian said you told him—"

"I lied."

"Oh ... "

60

Matthew considered this for a while in the darkness, thoughts about Monica whirling in his head, thoughts he couldn't understand. But he was happy she was with him. How could he have ever thought he could make it alone?

"Good night, Monica," he said quietly.

"Good night, Matt."

That night Matthew stood atop a huge rock tower in the desert. He was in full Hopi ceremonial dress; his hands were old and withered. He felt the creases in his face. And he began to dance...

15.

Jack Walker was an intuitive man. He had always known this about himself. Was he clairvoyant, telepathic, or psychic? Perhaps. In another place, at another time, he might have been branded a warlock or a wizard or a sorcerer. He had even been a subject of CIA experiments to measure ESP. The results were "inconclusive." But Walker knew he was special. For one thing, he had an astonishing ability to make good guesses. Remarkably good guesses.

Walker liked Robinson because he saw in him this same intuitive streak. And so he was not surprised when Robinson confronted him about their current investigation.

"Excuse my presumption, sir," Robinson began, "but I believe you know somewhat more about the nature of our investigation than you're choosing to divulge. I don't like being kept in the dark."

"Noted," Walker said dryly.

Robinson nodded. He got it. No secrets would be revealed today.

"I want data, Mr. Robinson. All the data you can get pertaining to the day in question."

"I'll put together a list of observatories. I'm sure we can yank data from NASA. Military satellites might be a source. I—"

"No, no. I'm looking for something else." Walker tilted his head back slightly. He seemed to Robinson to be almost literally sniffing the air for clues. "Start with power stations."

"Power stations?" Robinson asked, a little puzzled.

"Brownouts. Blackouts. Interruptions. Overloaded grids. Explosions. Fires."

Walker watched Robinson ponder this for a moment. "Why?" Robinson asked at last.

Because the signal was not a natural phenomenon, but a man-made one, Walker thought.

Because the signal did not come from space, but from Earth.

Because someone was sending up a flare.

"Just a hunch," Walker said.

16.

Matthew and Monica rented bikes.

"Harley?" the storeowner had asked.

"Schwinn," Monica had responded.

The desert landscape—rocks, crags, and hills—was beautiful and hypnotic. The sun was hot, but their canteens were full of water, and slowly they made their way toward the Hopi reservation and the mesas.

They stopped along the highway at all of the curio shops, each with an array of Indian-made items for sale. Most were cheap souvenirs; a few were finely crafted and expensive. They looked at all the jewelry, carved figurines, pottery, rugs, salt and pepper shakers, refrigerator magnets, postcards, and T-shirts for sale at each shop before casually showing the proprietor a photograph of Matthew's father, taken only weeks before his disappearance. Each time they were met with a blank stare and shaking head.

Every shop seemed to sell dreamcatchers, and Monica bought one, dangling it happily in front of her, a simple hoop with a web woven in the center, like a spiderweb, that somehow reminded Matthew of the electric sparks in Professor Schnabel's strange device.

"Better than a T-shirt," she said.

That night they built a small fire, off the highway, and spread their sleeping bags under the clear night sky. They ate sandwiches they'd bought that afternoon and fell into deep sleeps.

They arrived at the Hopi Culture Center at midday. It was a modern structure, built in pueblo style, on the Second Mesa. They entered through glass doors and found a young Hopi woman speaking to a group of tourists.

"Hopi is short for Hopituh Shi-nu-mu, which means 'the peaceful people,'" said the young woman. "For thousands of years we have lived on the Great Mesas, in small communities that reminded the Spanish explorers who first encountered them of villages they had left across the great ocean, and so called them 'pueblos.'

"Legend has it that we were guided to these lands by the Great Spirit, and it would be here that we would wait for the Elder Brother, a kind of a savior, who would come from the east to redeem the Hopi people. Some believed that the Elder Brother was the white man. Others, seeing the pain and suffering that the white man has brought, believe that the Elder Brother is yet to come." She smiled and added, "Of course, most Hopi don't believe in the old prophecies anymore."

Behind the Culture Center was one of the pueblos, a small village of adobe buildings. She led the group outside to the plaza. Everyone squinted in the sudden sun. A slight breeze swirled dust off the packed earth. The smooth brown walls seemed to soak up the light.

"That building is the kiva, the traditional ceremonial chamber, which has been built in this way by the Hopi for hundreds of years. Later today will be the Snake Dance, where the Kachina spirits leave the Mesa for their home in the mountains. They will not return until December when the cycle begins again."

"Will we be able to watch?" asked a young long-haired man in blue jeans and a tie-dyed T-shirt.

"Yes, the chief has decided the ceremony will be open to the public," she said. She noticed the camera around his neck. "But no photographs, I'm afraid." A collective groan went up from the small group.

"I'm sorry, but some Hopi still believe that photographs can be used to practice evil magic against them. You can take my picture, though."

The young woman continued talking for ten or fifteen minutes more, then posed for the promised photos, though she was dressed in nothing more exotic than a simple skirt and blouse. When the rest of the tourists trickled off to the gift shop, Matthew and Monica approached her. Matthew showed her the photograph of his father. She looked at it and shook her head.

"I'm sorry, I can't help you. I wasn't here seven years ago. I grew up in Flagstaff."

"Do you like working here?" Monica asked.

"I sure do. I like being in touch with my roots. Especially since it seems like nowadays Hopi kids spend most of their time playing video games."

She noticed the disappointed look on Matthew's face as he gazed at his father's photograph.

"Why don't you go see Bill? He runs the Culture Center. He's been around a while, and he's an expert on the Hopi Way. Maybe your father talked to him."

Bill's office was a sleek, modern affair overlooking the pueblo. Bill wore jeans and a sports jacket and looked very non-tribal, except for his straight black hair, which he wore long, in the traditional Hopi fashion.

He sat behind his desk, fingering the photograph of Matthew's father.

"I remember him," he said thoughtfully. His voice was low, with a trace of an accent. "He came here a lot. For a while anyway. It was some years ago, I don't remember exactly when."

"Seven years?"

"That sounds about right. Nice man. Clear eyes. Friendly. Very interested in the Hopi Way."

"What exactly is the Hopi Way?" Monica asked.

"That's a very important question, young lady." Bill settled in his chair. The room suddenly felt very still, and Matthew and Monica felt themselves leaning forward, as if Bill were about to whisper.

"The Hopi Way is potskwani. It is the right way of living, in harmony with the earth. Once the Hopi lived below the earth, in the Third World. But the people became corrupt. They forgot the ways given to them by the Great Spirit. They invented many destructive things. They became selfish and immoral. Eventually, they even came to believe there was no Great Spirit. They believed that they had created themselves. This was the time of koyannisqatsi."

"Life out of balance," said Matthew softly.

"You know of these things, young man."

"Just a little."

Bill continued with a gentle smile. "Some of the Hopi searched for a new world. A new beginning. They sent a prayer bird through the hole in the sky, asking for permission to leave that world. Then they climbed a reed through that hole in the sky and entered this world, the Fourth World, with the help of Maasaw, who is the caretaker of the earth.

"Maasaw gave the Hopi the potskwani, the Hopi Way, the way of balance with nature. This is the way we live. We use the earth, but we do not own it."

Matthew listened, wide-eyed, deep in thought. Some thread here, he knew, had interested his father. He needed to find what it was. He tried to think like his father, imagining him wandering in the desert, a white man among the Indians. Suddenly he knew.

"Who is the Elder Brother?" Matthew asked.

"Ah, that's what your father wanted to know. When the Hopi emerged into this world, the Elder Brother came with them. Then Maasaw instructed the Hopi to migrate to the Four Corners of the World. And the Elder Brother went away alone, to the east.

"The Hopi wandered until they saw a giant star. They followed it to their permanent home here on the Mesas. Here, the Hopi believe, the Elder Brother will return to them, to unite with his Hopi brethren. That day will be the Day of Purification, the end of the world."

Matthew was gazing off into the distance. His mind was racing. Now he turned back to Bill. "Why does the Elder Brother return? Why is that the end of the world?"

"The Elder Brother knows the way to the Fifth World. Legend has it that it is through a great kiva in the sky. Few believe the legend now, but your father believed it and was searching for it."

"Where was he searching?"

"North. Where the Anasazi dwelled, the Ancient Ones. Maybe Chaco Canyon. Maybe the Grand Canyon. Who knows? Why do you wish to know all this, young man?" Bill asked him, but Matthew was lost in thought, staring out the window at the pueblo, golden in the setting sun.

"His father disappeared seven years ago," Monica answered. "Matthew just wants to know what happened to him."

"Yes, I remember now," Bill said, getting up from his desk and walking over to Matthew. He put his hand on Matthew's shoulder. "Young man," he said softly, "I see you are full of feeling about your father. He seemed to be a fine man, and I grieve with you at his loss. But I caution you not to follow his path. Your father took these things, these prophecies, too seriously. These are just stories. Even here on the Mesas, the modern world has come. These new ways bring many good things. Your father believed in our stories more than we do. Only a few Hopi still wait for the Elder Brother, though a few of them, I believe, thought your father *was* the Elder Brother, was 'The One.'" Bill paused for what seemed like a long time. "And I fear," he said at last, "that your father may have come to believe it also."

"Believe what? That he was the fulfillment of a prophecy? That's crazy. My father wasn't like that," Matthew declared. He was confused. He felt as if he would burst into tears. His father was *not* crazy! He was *not*! But Bill seemed to be a good man, and he made sense. Matthew knew anyone would think so; one look at Monica's face confirmed that she did, too. She was looking at Matthew the way Mrs. Vines used to look at him when he was little and he woke up from a bad dream and ran into her room for comfort. "It's all right," she would say. "It's only a dream…" Had he forgotten that dreams are just dreams? When had he started to confuse dreams with reality?

Suddenly the professor seemed to Matthew to be just a crazy old man; all of Matthew's convictions to the contrary seemed to melt away. And if the dreams were just dreams, it meant one more thing: it meant his father was dead. Before Matthew knew what was happening, he began to cry.

Later, his eyes still red from the tears, Matthew walked with Monica through the pueblo. The sun was low in the sky, and long shadows stretched across the asphalt and the dirt lots, playing geometric shapes of dark and light on the low-slung buildings. Near the plaza, the sunlight seemed to bronze anything not yet in shadow. The air was still now and smelled of desert dust.

"Are you okay?" Monica asked, breaking their long silence. Matthew nodded, but said nothing. "Maybe you should call Mrs. Vines to tell her we're on our way home."

Matthew was still quiet.

"No. I can't go home," he said finally.

"Matt, I thought—"

"Dead or alive, I have to find out what happened to my father. We'll go north, toward Utah, toward the Canyons."

Monica didn't answer.

"I know it's crazy, but it's important to me. Bill said my dad went north, but the police never got past Flagstaff. No one has followed his trail that far. I have to go on." He could see that Monica was uneasy. "I need to find out what happened to him."

"All you'll find is a skeleton," she snapped. "I'm sorry, I didn't mean that," she added quickly.

"That's okay."

"You're right," she said, forcing cheer into her voice. "Anyway, it's on the way home. Sort of."

"Thanks," he said, at long last managing a weak smile. She took his hand, and they walked back to their bikes.

17.

Three black sedans snaked through the peaceful St. Louis sub
urb, Robinson and Walker in the third car, with Robinson driving. When they arrived at the target area, Walker radioed the
other cars to stop. They parked on a quiet street, lined with
trees moving gently in the summer breeze, surrounded by green
lawns, some watered by sprinklers. Robinson thought the green
surroundings made the sky seem bluer than usual, the cottony
clouds whiter.

"Now we work on foot," Walker said. The other four agents
got out of their cars. In their dark suits and sunglasses, Robinson
thought they looked conspicuously out of place. Ridiculous, really.
Movie stereotypes. And they made Robinson nervous. He didn't
know who they were, or even whom they worked for, other than
Walker. He didn't think they were CIA. They must be freelance
operatives, he thought. The fact that Walker had a private strike
force of his own made Robinson more than a little nervous.

Their mission continued to be a mystery. It had been a simple
task for Robinson to canvas utility companies, and the reports had
streamed in, faxed from all over the country. Walker had studied
these faxes intently, occasionally scratching out complex calculations on a note pad, before announcing definitively, "This is it,"
and handing Robinson a report of an unexplained power overload
knocking out a few neighborhoods outside St. Louis. To Robinson,
it had seemed as if Walker could just as well have been throwing
darts at a map.

"What exactly are we looking for?" Robinson asked as they got out of the car.

"I'll know it when I see it."

They found it half an hour later, agents swarming past the house-keeper and into the old house, flashing ID cards the poor woman was too flustered to read.

"Stop! Please! What are you doing? Who are you?" she sputtered, her head turning this way and that as several men infiltrated the first floor, and another bounded up the stairs.

"My word! My heavens!" The housekeeper was trying to decide whether to call the police, or whether these men *were* the police, when a tall dark figure with shoulder-length hair and dark glasses glided calmly through the front door, flanked by a handsome young man in blue jeans and a sweater.

"Excuse me, madam," said the man in the dark glasses. "To whom do I have the pleasure of speaking?" His polite manner, in such stark contrast to the commotion now occurring in various rooms of the house, disarmed her.

"M-M-M-Mrs. Sm-Smithers," she stammered.

"I see. My name is Walker. This is Mr. Robinson. We're terribly sorry for the inconvenience, Mrs. Smithers, but as you might have already surmised, we're here on an urgent matter of the utmost importance."

"Ah ... " she said, wide-eyed and a little breathless.

"Do you live here, madam?" Walker asked.

"She's just the housekeeper," said one of the agents, emerging from the living room.

Walker turned an icy stare on the agent. "I'm sure *she* could have told me that herself," he said. He returned his attention to the old woman.

"Whose house is it, then?"

72

"The professor's house."

"Professor?"

"Professor Schnabel."

"And where might I find Professor Schnabel?"

"He's in his workshop. But he really doesn't like to be disturbed."

"I don't think he'll mind."

The door to the workshop was locked, and even after prolonged knocking, there was no answer.

"Break it down," Walker said.

They forced the door open and rushed in, then stopped short.

"What in blazes is this?" one of the agents exclaimed. The huge apparatus dominated the large shed, soaring into the rafters.

Walker wrinkled his brow behind his dark glasses. "Mr. Robinson," he said. "Can you tell me what this is?"

Robinson shook his head. "I-I've never seen anything like it," he said, approaching the machine cautiously.

"Speculate for us, would you?" Walker asked.

"Well, for starters, I believe there's some sort of nuclear device at the center of it."

"Christ, it's a bomb!" one of the agents exclaimed.

Walker sighed deeply. "It's not a bomb, gentlemen. Now please be quiet and let Mr. Robinson do his job. And please don't touch anything!"

Robinson circled the thing warily, trying desperately to make sense of its intricacy. He approached the computer screens, staring at the data displayed on them.

"May I?" he asked Walker, gesturing to the keyboard.

"By all means," Walker said.

Robinson sat down and began typing commands. After a minute or so he leaned back in his chair, thinking.

"Is this the source of the power failure, Mr. Robinson?"

"Yes, sir."

"And the neutrino burst?"

"I believe so."

One of the agents approached Walker. "I think I've found the professor, sir," the agent said, motioning to the other side of the shed. There, sitting on the floor, his back leaning against the wall, head down, was an old man with gray hair.

Walker approached the old man and tried to rouse him with a hand to the shoulder. The old man's head rocked but remained bowed. Walker squatted in front of him, lifted the old man's head with both hands, and looked into his eyes. They were glazed.

"He's dead," Walker said simply. The old man seemed to be looking at something far, far away, his features frozen in a distant stare.

And he was smiling.

18.

We are at the base of a huge rock tower, looming high above us in the desert night. The full moon etches jet-black shadows on the cliff face, like shadows from an arc light. Above us, a lone figure on the flat top of the butte, arms outstretched, clothes rippling in the night wind . . .

We soar upward, the rock wall rushing past . . . and we are on the top. Our arms are outstretched. The wind rushes through our clothes, brings tears to our eyes . . . We see our hands . . . they are old and withered. We feel the cracks in our face . . . The moon above us now, too bright, too big, arcs across the sky, somehow accelerated. We can see the stars in their endless motion, swirling over us, time passing too fast, or maybe passing away altogether. The wind in our face seems to come from the very motion of the earth itself, rushing into eternity.

And we begin to dance . . .

Matthew's eyes snapped open from his dream. His first impulse was to look at his hands, though by the time he was holding them in front of his face, he'd forgotten why he needed to see them. To see if they were . . . But the dream slipped away.

He and Monica had spent the night outdoors in their sleeping bags, a little bit away from the pueblo, hidden behind an outcrop. After their meeting, Bill had offered to put them up in the Culture Center, but they'd told him they were traveling with Monica's family, choosing to lie, fearing if Bill knew they were traveling alone, he'd try to contact their parents.

In the morning, they headed north on their bicycles. They spent the day stopping at every ranch and shack, scattered and isolated along the northern reaches of the Black Mesa, sometimes biking miles off the main road under the hot desert sun. At each stop, Matthew would show the photograph, and in each case, the response was the same expressionless shake of the head; no one recognized his father.

They spent another night under the desert stars. The dreams came to Matthew stronger than ever, the fragments weaving themselves together: the cavern high in the cliffs, his father on the altar, and the dance on the flat top of the great rock tower.

The next day was much the same, and by the end of the day they were tired and frustrated. They were still biking north in the dusk when they came to an old Texaco gas station along the dusty, deserted highway. A light glowed inside as they rode up; through the window they could see a young man sitting with his feet up on a desk, napping. Monica sat down on the front steps while Matthew went inside. When she glanced over her shoulder a moment later, she could see the guy shaking his head no.

The last few days had been difficult for her. As much as she knew Matthew was on a wild-goose chase, she felt each disappointment as deeply as he did. She watched the growing intensity and frustration in his eyes and wanted to help him. But she didn't know how. All she could do was hope he'd come to his senses and accept the truth. And in the meantime, she was firmly resolved to stand by him.

Matthew came out of the gas station and sat on the steps next to her. They were quiet for a long time, both watching the vivid red glow in the west as the sun set. In the garage next to the main building, an old Indian mechanic was tinkering with the engine of a beat-up pickup truck, under a single, portable light slung from the open hood. Matthew pulled out his father's photo, thinking to show it to the man, then stopped, overwhelmed suddenly by a feeling of hopelessness, and tossed the photo on the concrete step.

"I'll never find out what happened to him, will I?" he said, half to Monica, half to himself. She didn't know what to say. They sat silently for a while longer.

"This place gives me the creeps," Matthew said finally. "What movie are we in now? Is there one called *Middle of Nowhere*?"

"I think that's an episode of *The Twilight Zone*," she said. "Anyway, even in the middle of nowhere, they still have Coke machines. I'm thirsty."

She walked over to the machine, an ancient red cooler vending the traditional glass bottles. "Look at this thing," she said. "It's a real collector's item. Only twenty-five cents, too." Monica searched her pockets for change, unsuccessfully. "Got a quarter?" she asked.

Matthew fished one from his jeans and flipped it to her. She slid it into the machine, heard the metallic click as the coin wound its way through the mechanism, pushed the button ... and nothing happened.

"Hey, no Coke!" she said.

"I think you have to open the glass and pull it out yourself," Matthew said. She tried yanking on one of the bottles. Matthew got up and tried. Still no Coke.

"No wonder it's only a quarter," he said, giving up and sitting back down. Monica gave the machine a few shakes and a swift kick. Nothing worked.

"Broken," said a deep voice, startling Matthew. It was the old mechanic, who had suddenly appeared behind them.

"No kidding it's broken," Monica said.

"Thirsty?" the man asked. His voice was calm and hypnotic.

"Yes," Monica said softly, as if she was falling under the old man's spell.

"I'll fix it," he said and approached the machine.

He stood in front of it for a few moments, then put his hands on it, as if to heal it.

Matthew watched the man standing motionless before the machine. His face was old and wrinkled, with chiseled features and deep-set eyes. It seemed to Matthew to be a noble face, wise, almost ancient. His hair was long and straight, in the traditional Hopi style. But his grease-stained overalls seemed wrong. Matthew imagined him dressed as a Hopi priest. And for just a moment, as Matthew daydreamed, the old face seemed oddly familiar, as if he recognized him from somewhere.

The mechanic closed his eyes, remaining still.

Suddenly, he opened the cooler door, grabbed a Coke, and in a smooth, slow, liquid motion eased it out of the machine. The bottle hissed as he pried off the cap, and he handed it to Monica, with a hint of a grin.

"Thanks," she said, surprised. She smiled back at him, but he looked away and approached Matthew, who was still sitting on the front steps. The mechanic stared at the photo of Jonathan Wilkes lying on the ground, then stretched out a bony finger and pointed at it.

"That man," the old Indian said slowly, "are you looking for him?"

"Yes," Matthew said. "He's my father." The old Indian closed his eyes again. "Do you recognize him? Have you seen him before?"

The old man remained quiet, eyes closed. He seemed to be thinking. At long last he opened his eyes. "He came here."

"He did?" Matthew asked.

"Many years ago," he intoned. "He came here many years ago."

"That's right!" Matthew exclaimed. "Monica! He remembers!" He looked back at the old man. "Can you tell me what happened to him?"

The Indian shook his head slowly. Matthew wasn't sure if he didn't know, or wouldn't say.

"Can't you tell us anything? Please?" Matthew pleaded. He felt close to something now, very close. The old man had to tell him. He just had to.

"Come with me," the man said.

"Come with you? Where?"

"I'll take you in my truck." He walked toward the garage.

"Wait a minute," Matthew said, but the old man had already started working again on the pickup, which seemed to be his.

"We've got to go with him," Matthew said.

"I don't know…" Monica said. She was feeling something, a sort of chill up her spine.

"I believe him, Monica. I don't know why, but I do."

Monica shook her head.

"Matt, can't you give this up now? I think it's gone far enough."

"What do you mean? We have to find out what happened to my dad. Something strange happened to him. I know it."

"I know you *think* you know."

"You mean you *don't*. You just think I'm crazy, right?"

Monica looked away from him, staring off into the night.

"Monica? Do you think I'm crazy?"

Monica sighed deeply. "No, I don't think you're crazy."

"You don't think I'm right about any of this, though, do you?"

"I just think you have an active imagination, that's all. And that you really loved your father, and that you can't really accept that he's gone. I mean really gone. Forever."

They stood for a while in a desert-night quiet broken only by the occasional metallic clanking coming from the garage.

"Why did you come then?" Matthew asked, breaking the silence.

"You're so dense," Monica muttered under her breath.

"Why, Monica? Why?"

"Because of you, you moron! I don't give a damn about your stupid father! I came because I wanted to be with you!"

Monica's expression was suddenly softer and pleading. Matthew was confused; his feelings were new, unfamiliar. He became suddenly aware of how beautiful she was. He wanted to speak, but all he could do was stare into her eyes.

"You go with the old man," Monica said. "I'm going home." She ran over to the bikes, jumped on hers, and took off down the highway.

"Monica, wait!" Matthew yelled. He grabbed his bike and rode after her. She saw he was following and swerved to a stop.

"What do you want?" she asked, a little breathless.

"You've got to believe me, Monica. This old man knows what happened to my father. I can't tell you *how* I know it's true, I just *know*."

"Don't you get it? I don't care whether it's true or not!" she said, putting one foot on a pedal as if to ride away.

"Don't leave, please." Matthew saw her hesitate, reacting to the emotion in his voice.

"Why not?"

"Because ... " he stammered. But he didn't know what to say or how to say it. Instead, without thinking, he grabbed her shoulders and kissed her. It was his first kiss. He didn't know that it was her first, too.

"Don't leave, Monica," he said.

"Okay," she said, and they stood for a while in the cool desert night, the luminous band of the Milky Way arching over their heads.

19.

Mrs. Smithers sat in the professor's study, her mouth pursed in anger and frustration as Jack Walker wandered about the room. The other agents were busy combing the house, and the sounds of their search—moving furniture, opening drawers, heavy footsteps— could be heard in the study. Robinson was still in the workshop, studying the professor's magnificent device.

Walker scrutinized the artifacts displayed in the various cases. Occasionally he held an object up to the light to see it better. He turned his attention to a row of dolls on a shelf.

"What a marvelous display of Kachina dolls," he said. "The professor must have had quite an interest in the Hopi."

"I wouldn't know," she said, frowning. "I was not involved in his work. You seem to know all about it, though."

"Oh yes. It's a great interest of mine. I regret not having had the chance to meet him. I've enjoyed his books over the years. I'm sure he and I could have talked for hours."

There was a loud thump from a room upstairs.

"Excuse me," Mrs. Smithers said, sounding exasperated, "but I demand to be told what is going on here!"

"I'm so sorry," Walker said calmly. "I know this is a bit of an intrusion. Tell me, have you seen what he was working on back in his workshop?"

"No. I never went in there. It was his private place. *I* respected his privacy," she said pointedly.

"Who else might have known about what he was building back there?"

"I really wouldn't know. He hadn't seen anyone for months. He just spent day after day locked up back there. He never let anyone in."

"He was ... obsessed?"

"Yes, obsessed. He was a brilliant man, you know, and brilliant people are sometimes like that."

"How long had this been going on?"

"I don't know. Ever since he left the university. Almost a year."

"Why did he leave the university, Mrs. Smithers?"

Mrs. Smithers sighed, resigning herself to this inquisition.

"Well, he hadn't really been himself for a while. To tell the truth, I wanted him to get some help—you know, psychiatric help—but he wouldn't hear of it."

"Not himself?"

"He seemed a little crazy at times. Or, not so much crazy as distracted. He was having trouble sleeping, and when he did sleep he had strange dreams. Lately though, I don't think he was sleeping at all." She paused, as if thinking of something.

"What are you remembering, Mrs. Smithers?"

"Nothing, really, it's just that I think he was never really the same after he lost Jonathan."

"Jonathan?"

"A young professor at the university. Jonathan Wilkes. He had been a student of the professor's, and he was the closest thing Professor Schnabel ever had to a son. The professor never married, you know."

"Never married. What a shame," Walker said, pulling up a chair. "He must have been lonely." The conversation was shifting in tone; suddenly they were like old friends.

"He was close to Jonathan, then?" Walker asked.

"Oh yes. Thought the world of him. What a fine young man he was, too. Handsome, very handsome. They were like two peas in a pod, those two. Always talking for hours, full of fantastic ideas. I sometimes thought Jonathan was crazier than the old man."

"And Jonathan ... passed away?"

"Oh yes, very tragic. The poor old man was crushed, don't you know. Having no family of his own."

"How very sad," Walker said, shaking his head in sympathy. "Tell me, how did Professor Wilkes die?"

"No one knows. He just disappeared. He went off into the desert somewhere, on one of his wild expeditions, looking for God knows what. Then he just disappeared without a trace."

Walker had a fixed expression; he was deep in thought.

"It's funny," Mrs. Smithers said almost to herself. Walker's head perked up, as if catching a scent.

"Funny? What's funny?"

"Funny how life works. I didn't think of it before, but Jonathan's son came by to see the professor just a few days ago."

"His son?"

"Yes. Nice boy. Hadn't seen him for years. Oh my, I really wasn't very nice to him, I'm afraid," she said, shaking her head, with her hand over her mouth. "But I've been worried about the professor, you know. I didn't think it would be good for the boy to see him; the professor's been very strange these last few months."

"He didn't see him then?"

"No, I sent him away ... though perhaps he snuck around back on his own. Hmm ... "

"What's the boy's name, Mrs. Smithers?"

"Matthew. Matthew Wilkes."

20.

The old Indian's pickup was a rusty rattletrap that once, in a past life, might have been painted blue. Matthew had to struggle to open the stuck passenger door before he and Monica were finally able to climb in, and now they were heading along a dirt road into shallow hills, bouncing around inside the truck on the barely upholstered seats, Monica getting poked by protruding springs.

"How old is this truck?" Monica asked.

"The engine's good," the old man replied.

"Right," she said.

"Where exactly did you say we were going?" Matthew asked, but he got no answer. Matthew turned to Monica.

"He didn't say," Monica said.

After twenty minutes or so, they came to a small adobe house on a flat spot beneath some small, rocky hills. They stepped out of the truck into the quiet night, bright with moonlight. Smoke came from the top of the house, and they saw a warm yellow light through a window. The old man went inside; Matthew and Monica followed.

Inside, an old woman worked over a fire in the center of the room. A pot of stew bubbled and steamed; she dished the stew out in wooden bowls and handed a bowl to the old man and two more to Matthew and Monica, along with pieces of flatbread. She seemed to have been expecting them, though Matthew couldn't figure out how; there was no phone, not even any electricity.

"You must be hungry," the old woman said to Matthew and Monica. "Eat."

They were, and they did, sitting on small stools around the fire. Matthew thought the stew was delicious; he asked for seconds, and Monica did, too. As they sat eating quietly, Matthew studied the old woman. She, like her husband, had a noble face, hard yet compassionate. Her straight black hair was tied behind her head with a leather strap. She wore a large, brownish dress, with small zigzag designs woven into the shoulders and a strap around the waist. He liked the way she looked, and he trusted her instinctively, as he'd immediately trusted her husband.

When they were done eating, the old woman took their bowls. The old man stood up and, without a word, walked out the back door.

"He doesn't say much, does he?" Monica said to the woman.

"My husband is a man of few words, it is true," she said. "But he is very wise."

"Excuse me, ma'am," Matthew said, "but we're not really sure why we're here. You see, I'm trying to find out what happened to my father." He handed her the photograph, and as she looked at it, he watched her face closely for some sign of recognition. But if she did react, he couldn't see it.

"I showed that photo to your husband, and he seemed to remember my father from years ago."

"I'm sure my husband will tell you more, when the time is right. In the meantime, I'll show you where you can sleep tonight."

She took them to a small room where they rolled out their sleeping bags on the floor, side by side. Monica fell asleep almost instantly, but Matthew lay awake in the darkness, thinking. After what seemed like hours, he heard the old man return. Matthew listened as the old man and his wife spoke in hushed tones, in a language Matthew couldn't understand. Then their voices blended into a dream where he heard their whispers echoing in the darkness, and his father lay on the altar again, staring at Matthew with eyes tired and infinitely sad.

They woke at the break of day and ate flatbread the old woman had just cooked on a smooth rock outside the house. She told them the bread was called piki. Matthew tried to ask about his father, but she would not discuss it.

"No questions now," she said.

Instead, Matthew went off with the old man to his garden, where he grew the corn that was their staple. He showed Matthew how to remove weeds from around the newly sprouted stalks. The sun was hot, but Matthew found himself enjoying the work, his mind emptying of the thousand questions keeping it a hornet's nest of activity. He slipped easily into the old man's rhythm, knowing as if by instinct what needed to be done—when to help the old man in moving one of the larger rocks being cleared for an expansion of the garden; when to go to the well for water for the corn, or for themselves; and when to rest. Occasionally, the old man smiled at him, but he did not speak.

They returned to the house for lunch, where they ate the piki Monica and the old woman had made that morning. Few words were spoken, and Matthew sensed that Monica had fallen into the same rhythm of activity with the old woman as he had with the old man. Her face had a tranquil expression, and her eyes, a faraway look. After they ate, Matthew and the old man returned to the garden, where the rest of the day seemed to fly by.

In the evening they ate again, comfortably around the fire. Matthew and Monica talked about the day's activities and felt somehow light at heart. The old woman joined in occasionally, but the old man remained silent, though his eyes gleamed, friendly and warm.

When they were finished eating, the old man filled the bowl of a pipe from a leather pouch and lit it. He puffed on it, then offered it to Matthew.

"No, that's okay," Matthew said. "Thanks for the offer, though."

"I want to try it," Monica said, reaching for the pipe, but the old man pulled it away.

"Wait a minute! Let me try!" she repeated, but the old man just sat with his arms crossed.

"It's because I'm a girl, isn't it?" she said. "I don't know if you've heard, but women these days have equal rights."

The old man handed her the pipe. She put it to her lips.

"Monica!" Matthew said. "You don't even know what's in it!"

"Tobacco," said the old man.

"See? It's fine," Monica said. She puffed on the pipe, drew the smoke into her mouth, and began coughing violently.

"Are you all right?" Matthew asked, slapping her on the back. Monica tried to nod, still gasping.

"*Strong* tobacco," the old man said, as Monica handed the pipe back to him. He flashed a hint of a smile.

"Very funny, very funny," she said, still coughing.

After dinner Matthew went for a walk with the old man. They walked along the rock ridge in the cool night air, but neither said a word. When they returned, they found Monica standing by the fire in the main room.

She had been transformed. Her hair was pulled back from her forehead and braided; her face was delicately painted. Around her neck was a black band, and from it hung a gemstone shaped like a teardrop. She wore a shirt with a beaded belt and leather moccasins halfway to her knees. Matthew stood and stared, speechless.

"Do you like it?" she asked, with an uncertain smile.

"I—I mean, it's … " Matthew stammered.

"It's a traditional Hopi costume for some sort of dance. I can't remember which one," Monica said. Matthew still couldn't manage to say anything. Monica seemed suddenly self-conscious.

"It's stupid, I know," she said, and her smile faded. She grabbed at one of the braids and tried to unravel it, then turned away and began wiping the paint off her face. Then she stopped, and Matthew realized she was crying.

"I'll never be pretty, I know it," she sobbed, trying to wipe her eyes.

"Tell her she's beautiful," said the old woman, who was standing in the doorway. "Tell her."

"You *are* beautiful, Monica," he said.

"Don't do me any favors, okay?"

"I'm not. I'm just not used to seeing you like this, that's all. And … I mean … oh, never mind."

"What?" Monica asked.

"It's just that if you start looking beautiful all the time, then all the guys will be after you, and I'll never be able to compete. I mean, let's be realistic, Monica. I'm really a nerd. Girls aren't interested in me. If you become like all the other girls, you won't be, either."

"Do you really believe that?" Monica asked, on the verge of laughing.

"Pretty much, yeah," Matthew said.

And Monica did laugh, and she was even more beautiful than before. The old woman stood the doorway, her eyes beaming.

"Come here, child," she said to Monica. "We have more work to do before we sleep."

Monica timidly approached Matthew and gave him a quick kiss on the cheek.

"You're such a moron!" she said and went into the next room with the old woman.

88

Matthew stood alone, confused. But his heart was beating fast, and he felt as if the fire was glowing within him.

21.

The scene at the Wilkes's home had been much like the one at the Professor's. Another housekeeper overwhelmed by a swarm of dark-suited men flashing ID cards, asking pointed questions, and infiltrating the house. Robinson felt sorry for the poor woman.

There must be a better way, he thought.

The housekeeper turned out to be the boy's legal guardian; Matthew Wilkes had no mother, and his father was presumed dead. She had raised him by herself for some years. She seemed to be a good woman, Robinson thought. She also had absolutely no idea where Matthew Wilkes had gone. She had, in fact, reported him missing the day before when she realized he wasn't spending the weekend at a friend's house as he'd claimed. She had already spent a day with the police and a sleepless night worrying. Now she verged on nervous hysteria. Robinson sat with her in the kitchen and tried to calm her down. He continued to muse on the puzzling questions his examination of the professor's bizarre contraption had raised. It all seemed to point to only one answer, but Robinson somehow refused to believe it.

And so Mr. Robinson and Mrs. Vines sat together, each preoccupied, and sipped their cups of tea.

Jack Walker, meanwhile, retraced the steps of a father and son. Sitting in Jonathan Wilkes's study, Walker pored through the professor's extensive materials, and a picture began to take shape in his mind. The threads of the various Hopi prophecies formed a pattern. He knew what Wilkes had been looking for; Walker had spent years searching for it himself. Walker suspected Wilkes might have found it. The legends were true, and the son was now following the father's trail. Walker would follow the boy. The boy would lead him to what he sought.

He went to Matthew Wilkes's room, wanting to better understand his quarry. He sat on Matthew's bed, surrounded by the boy's books, his star maps, and his telescope.

A precocious young man, Walker thought. And, Walker imagined, lonely. Walker's mind wandered, and he was sitting in another room, forty years past, in a small Midwestern town he had spent his whole life trying to forget. There he saw a boy named Jack Walker— lonely, alienated, friendless—drifting into the world of secrets that would become his whole life. In Matthew, he saw himself, and his heart was touched.

He shook himself from his reverie and went downstairs to the kitchen to join Robinson and the housekeeper for their third cup of tea.

22.

The second day with the old Hopi couple was much like the first. The quiet rhythm and tranquility of their life enveloped Matthew completely. At times he felt as if he'd always been there, could stay there forever.

Monica felt it, too. She found a sense of comfort there, a nurturing environment she'd never experienced before. Monica had never known her mother; she often wished she'd never known her father. Now, for the first time in her life, she felt what it might be like to have a real family. It was better than she could ever have imagined.

But she also felt a kind of foreboding, a sense that something bad was coming. They were waiting, she knew. Waiting for something to happen. But what?

"What are we doing here, Matt?" Monica asked that evening, after they had eaten and were sitting alone together by the fire.

"I'm not sure," he said. "They'll tell us when it's time."

"Time for what? We can't just keep living here. What about Mrs. Vines? She must have called the police by now. Even my father has probably sobered up long enough to notice I'm gone. They both must be really freaked out."

"I know, I know, but this is too important. We have to find out—"

"What do we have to find out?" Monica said. "Where your father is buried?"

"It's not just about my father."

"Then what is it about?"

Matthew stared into the fire, searching his feelings. "I don't know, I just know it's important, okay?"

Monica sighed, stood up, and turned toward the door. She bumped head-on into the old woman, who had been standing behind them. Monica was startled.

"You can't just sneak up on people like that," she said. "How long have you been standing there?"

"You are upset?"

"Yes, I'm upset. We can't just stay here forever. People are going to wonder what happened to us."

"You can leave whenever you wish," the woman said calmly.

"Oh yeah? Then tell us what we want to know."

"Monica, stop it!" Matthew said, but the old woman held up a hand to quiet him.

"What is it you wish to know, child?"

"Me? Nothing. It's Matthew who needs to know."

The woman turned to Matthew. "Why are you here, boy?"

"I want to know about my father."

"Why did your father come here?"

"I don't know."

"You don't know?"

"He was looking for something, I think."

"What was he looking for?"

"Why do you keep asking me?" Matthew asked. "If I knew, I wouldn't be here."

"Why *are* you here, boy?" the old woman asked again.

Matthew was getting angry. "What is this? Some sort of mind game? You're supposed to be answering questions, not asking them."

The old woman ignored Matthew's outburst. "Did your father call you here?" she asked. Her eyes seemed suddenly aflame. Matthew's head began to swim.

Yes, my father is calling me.

"Yes," he said.

The old woman stood silently, looking deeply into Matthew's eyes, considering his answer. Then she sat down next to the fire, her face half in shadow. The room was silent except for the crackling of the logs.

"What I will tell you," she said, "my husband would have me not tell, for he understands that to speak and to hear are not the same as to know. But I will tell you, because I know that to tell and to hear is your way, and because your father sought this secret, and because your mind, my boy, will not rest until you know it also.

"Long ago we entered this world," she continued softly, as if reciting a story told this way for countless generations, "through the sipapuni, the hole in the world, from the corrupted world below. Here we met the caretaker of the earth."

"Massaw," Matthew said.

"Yes," the old woman said, nodding. "Maasaw scattered ears of corn before the leaders of all the tribes that had emerged into the new world. Each in turn grabbed an ear, and each greedily grabbed for the longest ear. But one leader was not greedy; he waited, content to take the shortest ear of corn. And so Maasaw knew that this people could be trusted with secrets.

"He entrusted the Hopi with three things: the potskwani, which is the Hopi way, the navoti, which are the Hopi prophecies, and the Great Secret, which has no name. And so this humble people became, in their own way, caretakers of the world, for this Secret is not of this world, the Fourth World, but of the Fifth World. It is power over all things, the way to the Fifth World. This Secret has been kept for a thousand years. During that time, the Hopi have lived according to the potskwani and waited for the signs predicted in the navoti, the prophecies. For prophecy warns that men will come seeking this Secret, and with it, power over the earth, and that in those days the gods will no longer come to men, the world will become corrupt, and even the Hopi will forget the old ways. By these signs we will know that the Day of Purification is near. On that day, this world, the Fourth World, will end, and those who are not corrupt will enter the Fifth World."

"It's just a cycle repeating," Matthew said.

"Yes," the old woman said. "Maasaw knew those last days would be the most dangerous, and so he chose the Elder Brother of the Hopi for a special task: to travel to the east and sleep, waiting to be awakened by the cry of the Hopi when the Great Secret was most in danger. Then he would return to claim the Secret for Maasaw. On that day will come purification. For only the Elder Brother knows the way to the Fifth World."

"So ... " Monica said, thinking aloud, "if the Elder Brother will come, why is there any danger? Won't he just come and make everything okay?"

"No, child. The power cannot be taken away from anyone who holds it. It can only be freely given. Were an evil man to have that power, it could not be taken from him. And without it, there can be no entrance to the Fifth World. So you see, like everything in this world, the Sacred Thing can be used for good or evil; it is always our choice."

"What does this have to do with my father?" Matthew demanded.

"Your father was looking for the Secret Place, the kiva in the sky, the source of the power. And because he was a man, like all men he was tempted to use it for himself. The evil side can be very strong."

"My father wasn't like that!" Matthew said, suddenly upset. "My father was good. He believed in searching for truth, not power."

"All of us have two sides, right and left, good and evil. Your father had his evil side, and you do, too."

"These are all just stories, right?" Monica said. She turned to Matthew.

But Matthew was staring into the fire. Images from his dreams flickered through his consciousness like the flames.

"I dream of a great chamber; it *is* a kiva, I think. I dream of my father. He's lying on an altar. I have a knife in my hand. I stand over him ... and I'm afraid."

"Why are you afraid, child?"

"I'm afraid because ... because of the knife ... because ... " His voice trailed off. He was staring at the old woman, her face half-dark, half-light.

Left and right, dark and light, good and evil, he thought. His spine tingled. And he noticed the old man had entered the room and was standing over them, his eyes grave and serious. To Matthew he looked somehow ancient, like those stone figures on Easter Island whose origin and purpose were lost in the distant past. The old man stood silently for a long time. When he finally spoke, his voice came from a deep place.

"Time to go," was all he said.

23.

TRANSCRIPT OF CIA ARCHIVE VAS RECORDING 403/721.1 ABX
KVC 27JUL1322.27EDT

OPERATOR:ROBINSON/SUBJECT:WALKER/METHOD:WIRELESS

LOCATION:CLASSIFIED

ROBINSON: —to be informed as to the nature of our
current activity.

WALKER: Must you?

ROBINSON: I believe we are engaged in a rogue
operation, and you are acting without any authority
in this matter.

WALKER: I see.

<10.3 sec pause>

WALKER: Sit down, Robinson. Now, tell me what else
you think.

ROBINSON: There's a discrepancy in the time of the
neutrino detection.

WALKER: The time?

ROBINSON: We know when the professor's device
generated the neutrino burst. But that happened
after its detection in Australia. After, not before.

WALKER: Did it?

ROBINSON: Yes, sir. By several thousandths of
a second. I've checked and double-checked. The
detection in Australia comes before the burst itself,
which is, of course, impossible.

WALKER: Not impossible, since it happened. You mean you can't explain it.

ROBINSON: Yes. I can't explain it.

WALKER: You're assuming the neutrinos were traveling forward in time.

ROBINSON: Yes, obviously. What are you suggesting?

<6.7 sec pause>

WALKER: You know, Mr. Robinson, time is a funny thing. With the dimensions of space, we can move in all directions: up, down, away, toward, and so on. But we seem to experience time in only one direction. We call it past to future. Have you ever wondered about that, Mr. Robinson?

ROBINSON: I don't know.

WALKER: Of course you have. We all wonder about time travel. Did you know some physicists speculate that if and when the universe begins to collapse in on itself, time itself will flow backwards?

ROBINSON: No.

WALKER: The dimension of time is like a book. We read the story front to back, but we don't have to. We could read it back to front. Take our neutrino pulse, for example. It just follows a path in space/time. We're the only ones who care about which direction time is flowing.

ROBINSON: Wait a minute. You're saying the neutrinos were traveling backward in time?

WALKER: From a certain point of view. Imagine that the neutrino burst actually contained a message. What if the creator of the burst was actually the recipient of the message?

ROBINSON: I don't understand.

WALKER: If a tree falls in the forest, does it make a sound? The neutrinos might come into existence only if a device is in fact there to observe them.

ROBINSON: You mean the professor's device? So did it generate the neutrinos or detect them?

WALKER: An interesting philosophical question, in the end. It did send a message, however. When those astrophysicists complete their analysis, I expect they will discover that their neutrino burst was not a single event, but in fact a series of smaller pulses.

ROBINSON: So, the professor sent a message to the past? I thought time machines were only in the movies.

<4.8 sec pause>

WALKER: What if it wasn't the professor's message?

ROBINSON: Whose was it then?

WALKER: Someone long ago, perhaps. Someone who couldn't send the message themselves.

ROBINSON: I think I see. I want to write a letter to my great grandfather, but I don't have a time machine to send it. But what if I know my great grandson will invent one? I write the letter. And make sure it's kept safe until my great grandson can send it for me.

WALKER: Very good, Mr. Robinson.

ROBINSON: What kind of message?

WALKER: Maybe you just want your great grandfather to plant a tree. After all, it takes years to grow a tree. If you have to plant it yourself, you'll never live to see it full-grown.

ROBINSON: I'm sure this message wasn't about trees.

WALKER: No.

<5.3 sec pause>

ROBINSON: A warning maybe?

WALKER: Or perhaps a call for help.

ROBINSON: Yes. Interesting. An SOS. But sent backward in time.

WALKER: Received in the past.

ROBINSON: Many years ago. Light years away.

WALKER: Excellent.

ROBINSON: So that by the time the message is sent, help is already on the way.

WALKER: Bravo, Mr. Robinson. And if there exists a message that has already been received, then the sending of that message would happen by necessity. Indeed, must happen. Like predestination, if you will.

ROBINSON: Or the fulfillment of a prophecy.

WALKER: Exactly! Like a prophecy.

ROBINSON: Are you saying the professor was predestined to build that device?

WALKER: What if he was?

ROBINSON: Then the future already exists.

WALKER: Or?

<5.2 sec pause>

ROBINSON: Or is made to exist!

WALKER: Bravo, again. All you need is a very particular power.

ROBINSON: What power?

WALKER: The power to make dreams come true, of course.

ROBINSON: Do you actually believe that some Indians in Arizona have the power to turn dreams into reality?

WALKER: We're going to find out, Mr. Robinson. We're going to find out. Oh, and, by the way, you can turn off your recording device now. By the time they hear this, it will be too late.

24.

"We're not even on a road!" Monica exclaimed, looking out the window of the dilapidated pickup.

"I could have guessed that," Matthew said, bouncing wildly around on the front seat, sometimes high enough to bump his head on the roof.

They had been traveling for several hours, careening through the night landscape. At times Matthew thought the whole truck would simply fall apart into a pile of rusted metal. Monica had slept for a while as they drove, but the bumpy ride had jolted her awake.

"What time is it, anyway?" she asked.

"Two-thirty," Matthew said, checking his watch.

"It's late. Maybe we should stop for the night," Monica said to the old man. But he continued staring straight ahead as he drove, snaking his way around rocks and brush. They were running an obstacle course, and at high speed.

"Don't you think you're driving a little too fast?" Matthew asked. But he didn't expect an answer, and got none. The old man had not said a word since the three of them left hours earlier.

"It's kind of like a big video game," Matthew said, trying to lighten Monica's mood. A sudden dip threw them both in the air, then slammed them back in the seat.

"I'd say more like a ride in an amusement park," she countered. "Only dangerous."

"The moon!" Matthew exclaimed, gazing out the window. "It's huge." The moon was low in the western sky and seemed twice its normal size.

"I think it's a full moon," Monica said.

"Tomorrow night," the old man said suddenly.

"What?"

"The full moon is tomorrow night," the old man repeated, and Matthew suddenly felt uneasy.

In my dream the moon is always full.

The old man looked into Matthew's eyes, just for a second, as if reading his thoughts. But they both remained silent.

Matthew woke as the sunlight warmed his face. For a second he wasn't sure where he was, then remembered their drive through the desert night, and he wondered how he'd managed to get any sleep at all. They were stopped now, and the sun was just above the eastern horizon. On the front seat next to him, Monica was still asleep.

"Hey, wake up," he said, shaking her gently. She groaned in protest, then opened her eyes and squinted at the daylight.

"We're here," Matthew said.

"Where's here?" she asked, still groggy.

"Somewhere. I don't know. He said this is Navajo land. Anyway, we've stopped."

"Where's our tour guide?" she asked, noticing the old man was no longer in the truck.

He was sitting cross-legged on a rock, eyes closed. Matthew and Monica got out of the pickup and cautiously approached him. He did not acknowledge their presence.

"Now what?" Monica asked.

"Now we walk," the old man responded, without moving or opening his eyes.

"I can see why," Matthew said. He had moved past the rock and discovered they had stopped at the edge of some rocky cliffs dropping off sharply to a valley floor below. Driving was no longer possible.

The valley stretched as far as the eye could see, studded with enormous rock towers receding into the distance. It looked somehow unearthly. Monica had come up behind Matthew to have a look.

"Wow!" she said. "It looks familiar. I've seen pictures of this place before."

"And old westerns and TV commercials," he said. "It's Monument Valley." And as he stared out across the valley, he knew the rock tower in his dream was one of these great limestone buttes.

The climb down was difficult and dangerous. Matthew and Monica stayed close together as they descended, occasionally lending each other a hand, but mostly just calming each other's nerves.

"Shouldn't we have ropes or something?" Monica asked, halfway down.

"Or a net," Matthew responded.

"Or a parachute."

"Or a big vat of Jell-O."

At one point Matthew looked over his shoulder for the old man. He was well below them, climbing easily.

"How old would you say he is?" Matthew asked, grasping a ledge and straining to find another toehold.

"I don't know. He kind of looks a hundred."

"Yeah, but look at him!" Matthew said with amazement. The old man was as agile as a cat.

Monica was clinging to the cliff face, her cheek pressed hard against the rock. "I'd rather not look down right this minute."

It seemed like hours later when they finally reached the bottom. They found the old man sitting peacefully on another rock, smoking his pipe. He stared straight ahead, as if they weren't there.

"That was quite a climb," Matthew said. "You're in pretty good shape for a man of your age."

The old man said nothing.

"I can't believe we've done this," she said to Matthew. "We don't even know where we are. What if he leaves us? Or croaks? We'll never get back."

"He's not going to leave us," Matthew said. "I like him. I trust him."

The old man suddenly offered his pipe to Matthew. Matthew held up his hand in refusal.

"No, that's okay. We've been through this already," he said.

Monica again reached for the pipe. This time the old man handed it to her without hesitation.

"Monica! Not again!"

"I know what I'm doing," she said.

She drew on the pipe and inhaled slowly, staring into the old man's eyes. The old man remained expressionless. For a moment, her cheeks puffed up as if she was going to cough, and her eyes went wide. But she didn't cough this time, slowly exhaling instead.

She handed the pipe back to the old man, triumphantly. "See, nothing to it," she said hoarsely. She wobbled a little at the knees.

"Are you okay?" Matthew asked.

"Wow, that stuff goes right to your head." She noticed the old man smiling at her. "I know, I know, strong tobacco," she said. Then she plunked herself down cross-legged in the sand. Matthew sat next to her. Their eyes met.

The three of them sat quietly for a while in the morning sun.

"Now we walk," the old man said finally.

And they did.

25.

The six men sat around a large, rectangular table made of polished mahogany. Small spotlights cast islands of light in the otherwise dark room.

One of the men was speaking. "We don't have many details. We have confirmed the neutrino burst. It was detected in Australia six days ago. Obviously Walker has attached some great significance to it."

These remarks were directed toward an older, balding, white-haired man wearing small metal-rimmed spectacles. He sat quietly, his hands folded on the table in front of him, and sighed. The other five pairs of eyes in the room were now focused on him. There was a long silence before he spoke.

"Yes, yes ... well ... unusual ... Mr. Walker always has been a most unusual man, wouldn't you say?"

"Yes, sir."

"Odd and secretive," the white-haired man added.

"Yes."

"In fact, I would say that Mr. Walker has always been, well, inscrutable."

"Yes."

"What about Robinson?" the white-haired man asked.

"His file is in front of you, sir."

The white-haired man leafed through the file. The crisp papers made crisp sounds as he examined them, one by one.

"He seems like a reliable man."

"Yes, sir."

The white-haired man closed the folder in front of him. He leaned back in his chair, and his face seemed to recede into the darkness, except for the small spectacles, morphing into little white disks instead of eyes. He sighed again.

"Where do you think they're headed?"

"An Indian reservation, I think."

"What could this possibly have to do with Indians?"

"Unknown, sir."

"There are quite a few Indian tribes, I would imagine."

"About a hundred. We do know Walker's commandeered transportation from a military base outside St. Louis. He's headed southwest."

"Hmm … I'd say we'd better find out what he's up to." This remark met with five silent nods. The white-haired man smiled, and though his face was still in darkness, his teeth caught the light in an eerie glow.

26.

Through a long day, Matthew, Monica, and the old man trekked across the great desert valley. Huge sandstone buttes drifted slowly by them as they walked. All perspective dissolved in the sun and the heat and the expanse. Sometimes, Matthew thought, the towers looked no higher than a house and only a stone's throw away. Then they would seem miles high, the valley stretching for a thousand miles in every direction.

By mid-afternoon, Matthew was tiring. His feet burned from the desert heat. Monica, too, was suffering, her hair matted and sweaty, her eyes sunken in a perpetual squint. When their eyes met, she could manage only a strained smile.

But the old man seemed somehow changed, transformed by the journey, as if gathering strength with every step. There was a quiet energy in his face, and Matthew was reminded of Eastern mystics who could walk across hot coals in their bare feet without being burned, or sleep on a bed of nails without being cut. There should have been, he thought, something comforting in the old man's strength; the old man was obviously not going to "croak" as Monica had feared. Instead, Matthew felt a growing anxiety, not of being lost or abandoned in the desert, but a fear of reaching their destination—a fear of what they would find.

He glanced at Monica, hoping to shake himself out of his worry.

"Kind of a long walk," he said.

"You have a gift for understatement. My feet feel like they're about to fall off." She looked at the old man walking steadily ahead of them. "I don't know how he does it," she said. "It's like he could just keep on walking forever."

She suddenly sprinted to catch up to the old man.

"Excuse me," she said, "I was wondering what our ETA is."

The old man kept walking.

"Look, my feet hurt, and the rest of me feels like it's melting. And we haven't passed a Coke machine in quite a while. How long before we get there? Wherever *there* is."

The old man stopped and looked up into the sky. "Soon," he said.

"Really? Great! Because I don't know—"

"The storm is coming. Soon."

The old man suddenly began to chant, and his body began to sway. Then his feet began to move, and he danced.

"Hey, is this really the right time for this?" Monica said, shaking her head with exasperation. She turned to Matthew. "Can I have some water? My canteen's empty."

But Matthew didn't hear. He was watching the old man dance.

I've seen this before! His mind drifted to the cliff top in his dream. There, the wind raged and lightning slashed the sky, but he could see himself doing the same dance, as the storm boiled furiously around him. He could hear himself chanting the same chant.

Monica saw Matthew's trance-like gaze and felt a sudden rush.

There's a bond between these two, she thought. And if the old man was crazy, as she feared, then Matthew was in the spell of that craziness. She suddenly felt very alone and helpless. She'd been sure she could protect Matthew, be the voice of reason, whatever happened. Suddenly, she was not so sure...

She shook Matthew to snap him out of his daze. "Matt! Matt!"

Matthew's eyes came gradually back into focus. But when their eyes met, his expression was strange.

"He's right," Matthew said, dreamily. "A storm is coming."

"What are you talking about?" she said, gesturing to the bright, piercing blue above them. "There's not a cloud in the sky."

But Matthew spoke in low tones: "A storm is coming. Soon." The old man nodded slowly in agreement, his eyes wide and deep.

And for the first time since they had left home, Monica was truly afraid.

27.

It had been a long day at the little Texaco station; there hadn't been a customer for hours. No one had even driven by. The owner was on vacation in Vegas, and the old Indian mechanic hadn't been in for days. No cares, no worries, it was just the way he liked it.

And so the young man sat, feet up on the desk, chocolate-bar wrappers scattered on the floor and a fresh Snickers, half-eaten, melting in his hand, while his favorite country tunes crackled and hissed out of a small radio that usually had crystal-clear reception.

Sunspots, he thought, picking caramel out of his back teeth. He stood up, took another chomp on his Snickers and started adjusting the antenna. But the reception only got worse. Sometimes it got screwed up when a storm came, but the sky was cloudless blue, and the sun was dipping toward a clear horizon.

Time to get a new radio.

He was still fiddling with the dial when he heard the low sound of an engine in the distance. Sometimes, when the wind was right, he could hear the tractor-trailers coming from miles away. They almost always stopped at the little station, even if it was just to buy a bag of chips or a six-pack.

He craned his neck toward the window to look down the highway. The engine sound was getting louder, but the road both north and south was clear for at least a mile. His face screwed up in puzzlement, and he stood chewing and listening as the sound grew into a roar and the glass windows began to rattle.

And then, as if from out of nowhere, they appeared.

Helicopters. He stood dumbfounded as they touched down, just outside the window, a huge cloud of dust swirling up under them. Several men in dark suits scrambled out, heads bowed to avoid the whirling rotors. The attendant still stood slack-jawed as they charged in through the front door, bringing with them a rush of dusty air, scattering the candy wrappers like confetti.

"An old man work here?" one of the men shouted above the roar. "An old Indian?"

The attendant nodded, still speechless.

"Where is he?" the man shouted.

"Home, I guess," the attendant said with a shrug.

"Where's that?"

"Uhm ... not far ... you just drive down, I mean, if you had a car, that is ... Are you the police or somethin'?"

"Just tell us where he is!"

"Right, so you just follow that dirt road a few miles toward the hills."

Quick as a flash the men were out the door and scrambling back into the helicopters.

"You need some gas or somethin'?" the attendant called out after them, but by then the helicopters were already taking off.

"No gas ... " he muttered. "Stupid question."

The helicopters disappeared into the sky.

28.

Night was falling. Matthew, Monica, and the old man stood at the base of an enormous rock tower. The valley floor was darkening; only the top of the tower caught the last rays of the setting sun. Matthew looked up to take in the tower's enormity. And he knew he had seen it before.

"Are we here?" Monica asked. But neither Matthew nor the old man answered. The old man handed her some flatbread, and she offered some to Matthew, but he was far away.

"Matt?" she asked, giving him a gentle poke.

"We're here," Matthew said. "I've seen it in my dream. This is it."

Monica handed him some bread, which he took, and they both began to eat.

A wind was picking up, swirling sand and dry brush around them like a miniature tornado.

"I guess he was right about the storm," Monica said. "In your dream, is there a storm?"

Matthew nodded slowly; his mind was filled with images: the moon, the cave, his father calling for help, and . . . the knife.

"Matthew, I'm scared," Monica said. He looked at her. He was scared, too, but also excited. He suddenly thought of Christmas Eve and how he used to feel at the thought of Santa's arrival, when he still believed.

"What else happens in your dream?" Monica asked.

"I don't know. It's all hazy . . ."

She's scared enough. No need to tell her anything more. Besides, he thought, *nothing bad actually* happens *in the dream . . .*

The old man stood quietly, watching them.

"What now?" Monica asked the old man. But he remained silent, staring at Matthew, as if waiting for instructions. Matthew suddenly realized the old man wanted *him* to lead.

I'm in charge now. It's my dream…

The moon was up in the eastern sky, and it was full. Matthew watched the wind whipping through the old man's hair.

"Now we climb," Matthew said. And the old man nodded.

29.

"Who are you? Why are you here?" asked the old woman. She looked suspiciously at Walker and Robinson and the three helicopters idling behind them, rotors spinning at quarter speed.

"I'm sorry, ma'am. We don't mean to intrude," Robinson said. He flashed a badge at her. "Is your husband home?"

"No," the old woman replied. Robinson saw a flash of fear in her eyes. He was glad Walker had chosen to have the other agents remain on the copters.

"We're looking for a teenage boy," Robinson continued. "Accompanied by a girl. Have they been here?"

The old woman said nothing.

"They've been here," Walker said to Robinson. Then Walker began to speak softly to the old woman in a language Robinson knew must be Hopi. The old woman listened calmly, then replied in Hopi. Walker nodded.

For a long moment the old woman stared into Walker's eyes. Finally she led Walker to a niche in the wall containing a leather pouch. He picked it up to examine it. The old woman watched him intently.

"What is it?" Robinson asked.

"They call it a fetish bundle," Walker said. "It holds sacred objects." He unwrapped the leather and opened the pouch. Inside were quartz crystals, assorted carved-wood talismans, a small scroll, and a feather tied with a piece of string.

"This is a paho, a prayer feather," Walker said, showing it to Robinson. Walker seemed to handle the objects with reverence and understanding, and the old woman's expression became calm.

"And this," Walker said, replacing the feather and picking up the scroll, "is what we're looking for."

Walker unrolled the leather; it was old, very old, and somewhat faded. But the markings, in an ancient hand, made the purpose clear: it was a map.

Walker snapped a picture of the map with his cell phone, then rolled it back up and replaced it in the fetish bundle. Walker turned back to the old woman, and they spoke for a little while longer. Finally, Walker bowed his head slightly to her in a quick goodbye and walked out the door. Robinson followed.

"What did you say to her?" Robinson asked as they headed back toward the helicopters.

"Why, we just talked about the weather, Mr. Robinson." Walker paused and seemed to sniff the air. "There's a storm coming."

"Not according to the weather bureau," Robinson said, with a nervous laugh.

"There's a storm coming," Walker repeated, and, as if on cue, a gust of wind suddenly swept through.

Walker climbed back into the helicopter.

Robinson could see the other agents were as puzzled as he was. The helicopter engines revved for takeoff.

"What's going on here, Robinson?" one of the agents asked, shouting over the engine roar.

"I don't know," Robinson shouted back.

Moments later they were all back in the helicopters, then quickly airborne.

30.

They clung to the cliff as the wind swept across the rock face. Again, the old man climbed faster; Matthew and Monica climbed slowly and steadily and didn't try to keep up with him.

"I've never seen the moon so big!" Matthew said, staring up at the sky. "Look at it!"

"I can't!" Monica shouted back. "I can't look now!" She was clinging desperately to a crevice, trying to find a foothold. A rock gave way suddenly and clattered down to the desert below.

"Are you okay?" Matthew asked.

"No, I'm not okay! None of this is okay!"

"Rest for a second, then try again."

"Matt, I want to go home," she said.

"I know," was all he could think of to say.

Above them, the old man was moving effortlessly from ledge to ledge.

"How does he climb so fast?" Monica asked.

"I don't know," Matthew said, grappling for another handhold. The wind tore through him, as if it was trying to rip him from the face of the cliff. Clouds were rushing across the moon now. Even the moon itself seemed in motion; he felt he could see it arcing across the sky, could feel the earth spinning under him, as if the wind was spun from the movement of the cliff and the earth itself, racing through the infinite depth of space.

A few feet below him, Monica was still struggling when her second foot slipped. Suddenly she was hanging by her hands from the ledge, both feet dangling, face pressed against rock in terror.

"Matt! Help me!" she screamed.

Matthew could barely think. He looked for a way down to her, but there was nothing to grab on to.

He saw her hand slip and felt a jolt of fear. She was about to fall! As the rush of adrenaline kicked in, he saw that moment, that instant in time, with absolute clarity, as if time itself had stopped: the blaze of stars above them and the cold moonlight in Monica's hair; the panic in her eyes; below them, the desert floor, infinitely clear, as if he could see every rock and bush; a snake sidewinding through the sand; a coyote, eyes glowing, perched on a rock, surveying its kingdom. Matthew heard his own shouting voice as if from a great distance.

"Move your feet!" he shouted.

"I can't! I'm falling!"

Matthew was panicking now. There was nothing he could do to save her.

Suddenly, the old man climbed down past him and was next to Monica. But instead of helping her, he seemed to be talking to her. With the wind roaring, Matthew couldn't hear what he was saying.

"Grab her hand!" Matthew shouted to him. But the old man just stared into her eyes.

And then Monica's fear seemed to dissolve away. She took a deep breath, and after a long moment, she found a foothold with one leg, then pulled herself up on a ledge.

The old man quickly left her.

Monica climbed up next to Matthew. She grabbed him and hugged him, shivering.

"It's okay, Monica. It's okay," he said, stroking her hair. "What did he say to you?"

"He told me to be quiet. He said to let my foot listen to the rock." They sat for a while, halfway between heaven and earth, clinging to each other.

118

"Where is he?" she asked finally, looking up. The old man was nowhere to be seen. "Did he fall?"

"There's a cave just a little ways up. He's there by now, waiting for us."

"What cave? I can't see anything up there. How do you know there's a cave?"

"I just know."

They began to climb again, still shaky from their close call. But it was somehow easier now, and they were soon at the entrance to the cave, dark and forbidding, hundreds of feet above the valley.

"It's a cave in the sky," Monica said.

They turned back to survey the landscape. The moon was almost blinding. The great sandstone bluffs seemed to glow in the night and stretched as far as the eye could see. It looked, they both thought, like the surface of another planet.

"This is it," Matthew said. "I've seen it all in my dream. My father came here. He climbed, just like we did."

"I don't know much about geology," Monica said, "but it seems odd there'd be a cave up here."

"Maybe. Anyway, we've got to go in."

Matthew's mouth was dry with fear. He grabbed Monica's hand, took a flashlight out of his backpack, and together they walked into the blackness.

Once inside, they could see a reddish glow at the end of a long passageway.

"Where's that light coming from?" Monica asked.

"I don't know. The old man must have lit a fire."

Still clutching each other's hands, they moved cautiously forward. Lightning strikes outside flooded the tunnel with brief flashes of harsh electric light. Thunderclaps echoed off the stone.

As they approached, the glow became stronger, and as they followed the passageway around a bend, they discovered its source: dozens of torches on the walls ahead of them.

"Did the old man light all these?" Monica asked.

"I don't know."

The sound of the storm was well behind them now, and they could hear the faint sound of voices.

"Listen," Monica said, squeezing his hand tightly. "There are lots of people here. They're chanting. Can you hear it?"

But Matthew didn't answer; he was staring at something lying against the cave wall. It was old and dirty, but he recognized it immediately. He crouched down.

"What is it?" Monica asked.

"A backpack. It's my father's."

"Are you sure?"

"Positive. He was here! My father was here!"

He unzipped the pack. Inside was a notebook containing diary entries, a compass, and an old laptop. There were maps, most of them of the Southwest, full of calculations his father had marked in pencil. And there was a wallet with his father's driver's license. Then he found a picture of himself when he was five and another of him sitting on his father's shoulders, taken on a trip to the zoo that suddenly flooded into his memory and brought a lump to his throat.

The chanting seemed louder now.

"Let's go in," Matthew said, his eyes wide in the flickering torchlight.

"I have a feeling something is wrong, Matthew. Something bad is happening here. Maybe there are some things in life we don't need to know."

"I've been called to this place, Monica. I don't know how or why. But my father called me and I have to go in. You can wait here."

"No. I've come this far. I'm not leaving you now." She grabbed his hand again. They walked slowly toward the light and emerged from the tunnel. What they saw left them dazed.

They had entered a huge cavern. Its stone floor and walls were completely smooth and arched above them so far that they receded into complete darkness. Matthew could not even guess at the height of the ceiling. But it was as if the whole top half of the great rock tower was hollow. The chanting reverberated through the space, and Matthew felt as if he'd entered some enormous cathedral.

"Look at the size of this place!" Monica said. "It's incredible!"

"I've never seen anything like it," Matthew said. "It's the secret kiva, the kiva in the sky."

"No caves are like this," she said. "Look how smooth the walls are. It doesn't seem natural at all."

"No, it doesn't seem natural," Matthew said, and in a flash he knew ... he knew!

"Could the Hopi have made this place somehow?" she asked, thinking out loud.

"No. Not the Hopi."

"Who then?"

Matthew suddenly felt a hand on his shoulder and spun around. The old Indian stood in full Kachina dress, red-and-white robes with a white sash, feathers at his shoulder and on his head. He smiled at Matthew, a wise, ancient smile.

"Now you understand," the old man said, quietly. His eyes seemed to shine with the deep mysteries of the universe.

"They're coming," Matthew said.

"Yes," the old man said, nodding. "They're coming."

Matthew noticed the circle of men on the other side of the huge chamber; they were chanting, and in full ceremonial dress. The old man walked toward the circle, and Matthew and Monica followed.

As they approached, some of the men moved aside to reveal a stone slab, like an altar, and lying on the stone slab, a man.

Matthew approached the prone figure and began to shake. At first he thought he was looking at a corpse, like in a funeral scene in a movie, where there was an open casket. In movies, though, the eyes were always closed; here, the eyes were open. And in those glazed eyes Matthew didn't see death; he saw pain and suffering and a great sadness.

"Who is he?" Monica asked nervously.

"He's my father."

31.

"Gentlemen, what I'm about to tell you may sound somewhat, er, fantastic," the young man said. He was standing at the end of the large rectangular table, around which sat the six men. Again, the focus of attention was the middle-aged, balding, white-haired man with the round spectacles: the Director. Eighteen hours had elapsed since their last meeting.

"Seven days ago," the young man began, "at a particle physics research facility in Australia, a powerful burst of neutrinos was detected. Neutrinos are subatomic particles with very little mass. They can pass through practically anything, so they're normally very difficult to detect." The young man tugged at his necktie, cleared his throat, then continued:

"News of this detection came to the attention of Jack Walker, who immediately saw in it a certain, shall we say, significance. Deputy Director Walker has been engaged in a rogue operation since that information reached him. We know now, in fact, that he personally traveled to Australia to confirm the detection and, I believe, to gather specific data about it. He accomplished this, by the way, by impersonating an Australian astrophysicist."

There were chuckles around the room. "I would love to have heard his Australian accent," one of the men said, and the young man smiled meekly.

He continued, "The scientists in Australia were looking for the source of a signal they assumed had come from deep space. Walker, however, seems to have guessed, somewhat brilliantly, I might add, that the source of the signal was terrestrial."

"Man-made?" asked the Director.

"Yes. Which is interesting, of course. As you know, we do look for these kinds of phenomena. As evidence of secret weapons research, for example."

"I gather that is not the explanation in this case."

"No, sir, it's not. In fact, Walker managed to isolate the source in remarkably short time. It was, in fact, some sort of device, I guess you'd call it, built by a university professor, just outside of St. Louis. In his garage."

"You're kidding," said several agents at once.

"I know it sounds ridiculous, but we've seen the thing. It is, um, unusual, to say the least."

"Unusual enough to have produced the signal?" the Director asked.

"Well, among other things, the professor seems to have built a nuclear reactor in his backyard. And a good one, too. We've never seen anything like it."

"He's a physicist?"

"Anthropologist."

"You're kidding."

"I wish you'd quit saying that. Obviously, I'm not. I told you this was strange stuff. The professor, whose name was Schnabel, by the way, was a specialist in tribal cultures."

"Was?" asked the Director.

"The professor was found dead, in the shed behind his house, with his contraption."

"And Walker?"

"Oh, Walker had been there, all right. The professor was already dead, though. The strain of building the thing seems to have simply burned him out."

"You say the professor was an expert on tribal cultures. I assume Native Americans fit that category."

"They do. Of interest here is that among his many interests and areas of expertise, it turns out Jack Walker is also an expert on tribal cultures."

"How do you know that?"

"It's in his file. Actually, there are a number of interesting things in his file, including a proposal for a study of tribal legends and prophecies. He had this idea twenty years ago, and I assume since then he has conducted some research on his own."

"Looking for what?"

"Secret knowledge. Secret powers. Whatever."

"That's ridiculous," one of the agents grumbled.

"No more ridiculous than the ESP experiments we've conducted for decades. And not just us, but everyone—the Russians, the Chinese, the Israelis. Anyway, we've been looking at the professor's device for twenty-four hours now, and I can tell you, the boys we have out there in St. Louis can't make heads or tails of it. It's of a design so far beyond our technology it seems, well, like magic."

There was a commotion in the room as violently dissenting voices chimed in; the Director quieted the room with a raised hand. He leaned back in his chair. There was silence for what seemed to everyone there like a long time. Finally, he spoke. "Let me see if I follow this," he said in a voice so calm and quiet it seemed more like a whisper. "There is an Indian tribe in the Southwest in possession of some great, for lack of a better word, power. Or knowledge. In any case, something which made it possible for the professor to build his ... thing. Am I with you so far?"

"Yes, sir."

"Jack Walker is on a quest for this power?"

"I think so."

"Obviously, then, the old professor did not actually possess it himself. The power, that is. Are we talking about another device here? Or a book of some kind? What exactly would this power be?"

"I don't know. I suppose it could be some sort of device. If it is, then you're right, the professor didn't have it, though he may have been somehow controlled by it."

"Controlled?"

"It is my understanding the professor had not been himself for some time. Presumably while he built this device. That could imply some sort of mind control."

One of the other agents could no longer contain himself. "Excuse me, sir," he said, addressing the Director, "but this is crazy. I can't believe we're expected to take these fantasies seriously!"

The Director smiled. "There are more things in heaven and Earth than are dreamt of in your philosophy, my friend. Now please be quiet." He turned back to the young man giving the briefing. "Please continue. This is most interesting."

"The rest is just wild speculation."

"The floor is yours," said the Director with a gesture of his upturned hand. "Speculate away."

"It seems that seven years ago a former student of Professor Schnabel disappeared while on an expedition in Arizona, where Walker seems to have gone. This man, Jonathan Wilkes, was investigating some legends and prophecies of the Hopi. The Hopi reservation is in northwestern Arizona, where they've been for hundreds of years. They live on three Mesas there, in pueblos, or small villages.

"It's difficult to sort through all of this; the Hopi have an elaborate set of gods, legends, prophecies, secret religious ceremonies, and so forth. But I think Wilkes's interest centered on a great secret referred to in a prophecy Walker cited in his proposal. The nature of this secret is never discussed. It was told to the Hopi by the caretaker of the earth."

"A god."

"Yes."

"And if that god were not actually a god, but perhaps, an extra-terrestrial ..." The Director's voice trailed off.

"Then the legend might be true. The secret, whatever it is, might actually exist."

The room was suddenly silent.

"This is a joke," said someone, breaking the silence.

"Is it?" said the Director. "Jack Walker doesn't seem to think it's a joke."

The young man continued. "Imagine, just hypothetically, an alien stranded on Earth. Maybe in a crash. Who knows? Maybe he just runs out of gas. Anyway, he has some powerful, I don't know, thingamajig with him, weapon maybe, some element or elements of their technology, which we're assuming, for the sake of argument, involves the capacity for interstellar travel. In other words, very, *very* far ahead of our technology today. This thing must certainly be dangerous. He can't just leave it lying around. So anyway, here he is stranded on Earth, with no way to leave, and maybe, for whatever reason, no way to signal for help. What would he do? Maybe he would give this thing to someone he knew would protect it after he died. Someone who would guard it and keep it secret until Earth technology made it possible to send a signal home."

"The professor's device," said the Director.

"Yes. It seems as good an explanation as any. Maybe that device was an attempt to call for help. Before this weapon, if that's what it is, falls into the wrong hands."

"Jack Walker's hands," the Director said.

"I'm sure this is what he's after, sir."

The Director nodded again.

"Wait a minute," one of the other agents said, shaking his head. "Do you really believe any of this? Do you really believe something bad is going to happen if Walker finds what he's looking for?"

"I believe," the young man said, leaning on his arms with his palms pressed to the large table, "that if Jack Walker finds what he's looking for, it will change the world ... forever."

32.

Matthew had dreamed about this moment every day since his father's disappearance seven years earlier. He'd wanted to believe, needed to believe, that his father was still alive. For years he'd imagined the excitement he'd feel when he saw his dad again, never losing hope that one day his father would come walking through the front door with a grand story to tell.

But now, with his father lying before him, half-alive and half-dead, he felt no jubilation, no joy. Instead, fear built in the pit of his stomach, the same fear he'd felt in his dreams, night after night. But this was no dream. This was really happening.

"Is he alive?" Monica asked, grabbing Matthew's arm.

"I think so," Matthew said. He looked at Monica and saw a kind of dread in her eyes. Then he looked around at the rest of the Hopi men; they were all simply staring at him, expectantly.

"What's wrong with him?" he asked the old man, who was standing quietly with the others. "What happened?"

"The power is not for men," the old man answered. "He is at war with himself."

"At war with himself?"

"Your father holds the Secret, but he does not master it. Now he does not eat or sleep. He does not live; he does not die."

"Can't you help him?"

"It cannot be taken from him. It can only be given freely, and part of him will not give it up. All men have two sides, and in him the two sides still struggle."

Matthew shook his head in confusion. "I don't understand! There must be something you can do!"

"He called *you* here," the old man said, suddenly sounding angry. "*You* are the one. Only you can help him."

"But I don't know what to do!"

Suddenly Matthew felt a hand on his shoulder spinning him around. One of the younger Hopi men held him tightly and stared into his eyes. Matthew looked to the old man for help.

"He questions your wisdom," the old man said to Matthew.

The young man grabbed Matthew's arm and thrust a dagger into his hand.

Like the dream!

Matthew stared at the knife in his hand, shining in the firelight.

"He's my father! I won't kill him!" he said to the old man, pleading. But the old man just stared at Matthew, saying nothing.

"Let's go get help!" Monica said. "We can get a doctor."

The old man grabbed Monica and pulled her away from Matthew. "Do not interfere," he said to her. "He must choose."

Matthew felt far away now, as if in a daydream.

"I don't think a doctor can help him," Matthew said.

Suddenly, his father's eyelids fluttered. Matthew leaned down.

"Dad? Can you hear me?"

"Matt? Is that you?" his father asked, his lips barely moving.

"Yes, it's me."

"Son ... help me."

"What should I do? I don't know what to do!"

His father struggled to speak, and Matthew put his ear next to his father's lips.

"The crystal ... use the crystal," his father said. Then his eyes closed again, and he fell silent.

"Crystal? What crystal? Where?" he said, shaking his father gently, but he didn't answer. It was at that moment he saw it: his father's hands were folded across his chest, holding something between his clasped fingers.

"What is it?" Matthew asked the old man.

"The Secret," the old man answered. "He offers it to you."

"Is that what's making him sick?" Matthew asked. "If I take it, will he get better?"

"The power is not for men," the old man repeated.

"Will I get sick?" Matthew asked, but this time the old man said nothing.

"Please, Matt," Monica urged. "We've got to go get help." She struggled to get free of the old man's grip, but he would not release her.

"My father called me here," Matthew said to her. "I have to." He turned to his father. "Dad, give it to me. I'll take it." At first, his father didn't move, but after a moment he slowly turned his hands upward and opened them. Cradled there was a crystalline object something like a teardrop, though much larger. It was jet-black, and at first it seemed smooth, but as Matthew looked closer he could see it was many-faceted, like a diamond, though the surfaces seemed somehow not to reflect light but to absorb it. Light came from within the crystal, as if from a great depth, and as he gazed into it, Matthew's thoughts began to drift; he felt for a moment like he was plunging into the heart of the crystal itself.

He jerked his thoughts back and looked into the old man's luminous eyes.

"Please, Matt, don't!" Monica said. Matthew felt a rush of love for her that made him shiver. Then, in one motion, he turned back to his father and took the crystal.

It felt neither hard nor soft, not hot, not cold. In fact, he couldn't really feel it at all. His hands felt as if they weren't his, but someone else's. For a moment, he thought he was dreaming. He imagined waking up again in his bedroom, as he had so many times before. But the image of his home melted away, and the crystal in his cupped hands seemed to grow larger, to draw him in. The cavern became a blur, and the crystal enveloped it, and him, too, as if he were now inside it, though he could still see it in his hands. His hands became old and decayed, then bony, the hands of a skeleton, cradling the crystal, which had become the whole earth. And his fingers became powdery and spun themselves into fine latticework, like a spiderweb, stretching infinitely through time and space, drawing in the sun and the moon and the planets and all the multitude of stars and galaxies in a great eternal whirl.

And as he felt himself rushing toward the end of time, thoughts of his life, so small and brief, fluttered around him like feathers, like the petals of a flower scattered to the wind. Images came to him as if from an ancient place, memories of things that happened so long ago that such a length of time could not be measured. And the voices of his past swirled in his head:

—You are the one—

—I don't understand—

—They're just dreams, Matt—

—BUT THE DREAMS ARE REAL! —

—The secret! Must I tell you everything? —

—The power is not for men—

—Am I normal? —

—There are enough normal people in the world—

—You are the one . . . the one—

—Enough normal people in the world—

—Just dreams . . . just dreams—

—But they're REAL! —

—When are you going to learn that you don't need your father? —

—I love you son, always remember that—

—You don't need your father! —

—I love you son—

—My father—

—I love you . . .

. . . I LOVE YOU, DAD!

And the earth in his hands became the face of his father.

33.

Matthew felt as if he were waking from a dream. For a moment he didn't know where he was. Then the world became solid around him again; he was still in the cavern. And he was in his father's arms.

"Matthew? Are you all right, son?" his father asked, hugging him tightly.

"Dad! You're alive!"

"I'm fine, son, thanks to you."

"I can't believe it's really you!"

"Well, I can't believe it's you either!"

He hugged his father back.

"You did it, son. You saved me. I knew you could."

"What happened to you?" Matthew asked. He was still a little dazed, and his head felt heavy, as if it were stuffed with cotton. "I remember I took the crystal ... and then I was somehow very old, older than time somehow, and the whole world seemed small, like a toy..."

"It was just a dream, son. The crystal makes you dream. I don't really understand it myself, but I used it to call you here."

"An extraterrestrial left it here. That's what you figured out, isn't it, Dad?"

Jonathan Wilkes smiled broadly. "You always were pretty sharp, Matthew. That's exactly right. A long time ago. A small group of Hopi have kept it ever since. They knew it was dangerous, but I was foolish. I had to try to understand it."

"What did the crystal do to you?" Matthew asked.

"It was like a bad dream, son. A bad dream you can't wake up from. I needed someone to wake me, and I reached out to you. I knew you could save me."

Matthew looked at the crystal in his hand. It no longer seemed to glow. It was just a lifeless piece of glass.

He felt Monica's hand on his arm.

"You did it, Matt! You were right," she said.

"And who might this be?" asked his father.

"Monica Jordan, sir. I'm a friend of Matt's."

"Well, if you've come all the way here with him, you must be a good friend indeed."

Matthew nodded, but his thoughts were wandering. Something didn't seem right.

"Son? Are you okay?"

"I—I feel a little lightheaded, that's all."

"From the crystal. It will wear off soon enough," Jonathan Wilkes said.

The old man and the other Hopi were staring at Matthew, silently. Their eyes made him uneasy. They seemed to be studying him, as if waiting for something to happen.

Something is wrong, Matthew thought. *There's something I'm forgetting...*

"What about Professor Schnabel?" Matthew asked at last.

"Professor Schnabel? What about him?"

"He dreamed about you, too."

"Did he?"

"He said you told him to build some strange machine."

"When did you see Professor Schnabel?" Matthew's father asked.

"Before I came to look for you. I thought he might know something about what you were working on. He said he had dreams about you. And you told him to build this strange device. And he really built it. I saw it!"

"That's strange," Matthew's father said, shaking his head slowly. "I don't know…"

"But how could you not know? Weren't you calling him, like you were calling me?"

"I don't think so. It's not important anyway. Theodore always was a little crazy. Who knows what wild notion he got into his head." Professor Wilkes put his arm around Matthew. "Let's go home, son."

Monica slipped her hand into Matthew's, and the three of them began to walk toward the passageway that would lead them out.

But the old man stood motionless, transfixed, staring at Matthew.

Everything's okay, Matthew told himself. *We're going home.*

Suddenly, he remembered the crystal, still in his hand. "Dad, what about the crystal?"

"Oh, I almost forgot," his father said. "It needs to be studied, so I guess we should bring it to the university."

"That seems like a good idea," Monica said, sounding cheerful. But Matthew thought he heard something else in her voice, something… different…

"But what if it's still dangerous?" Matthew asked.

"It's not dangerous anymore, son. Here give it to me. I'll carry it." His father stretched out his hand.

Matthew turned the crystal over in his fingers thoughtfully. It still seemed cold and inert.

Why am I worried? Dad's right, it doesn't seem dangerous…

"Are you sure it's okay?" Matthew asked.

"I'm sure."

Matthew looked back for reassurance. The old man's eyes were steady and penetrating. Matthew glanced down at the crystal, then at his father's waiting, outstretched hand.

"Maybe we should leave it with them. With the Hopi," Matthew said.

136

At this, his father just shook his head gently. "No son, just give it to me."

Matthew did not move; he felt frozen.

"Matthew, give it to me," his father repeated, his voice sterner.

Matthew searched his father's eyes. They were distant.

"Give me the crystal, Matthew," his father intoned with authority.

Monica squeezed Matthew's hand. "What's wrong, Matt?" she asked.

Matthew couldn't make a sound. Again it was as if he were dreaming, fear rising in his throat. Monica squeezed his hand again.

"I want to go home, Matt. Just give him the crystal," she said. Matthew was sure he heard something dark, almost evil, in her voice.

"It's all right, son. There's no danger. *Just—give—me—the—crystal.*" His father's voice was hard now, his eyes steely.

Matthew froze. Why was his father acting this way? And what were the old man and the other Hopi waiting for? Everything *looked* normal, and yet somehow he felt things weren't what they seemed. He couldn't put his finger on it.

"Give him the crystal, Matt," Monica said, with a big smile. "Your father knows what's best."

And in a flash, he knew.

Monica, the *real* Monica, the Monica he knew, the Monica he loved, would never say that. Ever.

The person standing before him was *not* Monica.

"What did you say?" Matthew asked her.

"I ... I ... " she stammered.

Matthew looked back at his father, and his father's face seemed suddenly demonic, his eyes angry flames.

"Give it to me, you little brat!" his father shouted.

"No!" Matthew said. *"No!"*

At this his father clenched his fists. His body began to warp and twist, as if he were changing into some hideous monster. Matthew felt a sudden jolt of terror and remembered, for a crazy moment, the night he and his father stayed up to watch *Dr. Jekyll and Mr. Hyde* on the late show.

Just like a movie . . .

Matthew looked at the crystal, now glowing. The room dissolved around him again, and for a moment, all he could see was the crystal. Then he heard Monica's voice, screaming, "Run, Matt! Run!"

Suddenly the cavern materialized around him again. But this time, Matthew was lying on the stone altar, and his father was standing over him, holding a dagger to his throat.

"Matt!!" Monica screamed again. She grabbed Matthew's father and tried to pull his arm away. Matthew rolled out from under the blade just as his father thrust it down. He felt a burning slash at the side of his neck, and then he thudded to the cavern floor. He scrambled quickly to his feet.

Matthew struggled to understand what was happening to him. It was the crystal, he knew. Matthew felt as if he had been jolted out of a daydream. But the dream had felt so real. And what if he had not snapped out of it?

"Matthew! Give me the crystal!" his father barked, coming after him again with the knife.

"No!" Matthew shouted, backing away. He looked at the old man, who nodded.

"They're coming," the old man said.

"Will they take it back?" Matthew asked. The crystal was warm in his hand.

"They will not *take* it. It is too powerful. It must be given."

"Then I'll give it to them," Matthew said, and he dashed out of the cavern.

138

34.

Matthew emerged into what seemed like a gale. Without thinking, he started climbing toward the top of the cliff.

This time, he moved with confidence up the stone face. He looked down to see his father was climbing after him, but with a struggle. He could see his father shouting, but the roar of the wind smothered all sound.

When he reached the summit, Matthew sprinted across the flat top of the great stone tower.

They're coming. They're coming.

Without thinking, he began to imitate the old man's dance, stretching out his arms toward the full moon above him, the wind ripping through his clothes.

Now is the time! Come now!

"Matthew!"

He whirled to face his father.

"Don't be stupid, Matthew!" his father yelled over the wind. "Give me the crystal!"

Matthew felt the crystal pulsing. Was this a dream, too?

"You're not my father. You can't be! You were going to kill me!" Matthew touched his neck, and when he looked at his hand, there was blood.

"For a higher purpose, Matthew! Don't you understand the power of that crystal? The good it can do for mankind? It's worth any price, even your life. Even mine."

The crystal was hot now, and Matthew understood.

It makes dreams come true. But his father had not been able to control it. So he had used Matthew's own thoughts to spin an illusion.

"I *am* your father! I *am*! Now give me the crystal!" Jonathan Wilkes said, moving closer to Matthew, brandishing the knife.

It makes dreams come true. But Matthew knew this was no dream. He had the crystal now. He would not let his father deceive him again.

"No! I won't give it to you! And you can't take it from me."

They stood face to face, like gunfighters in the Old West.

It makes dreams come true. Everything you could ever wish for … The possibilities were endless, Matthew realized. He could have all the friends he could ever want. Maybe a new bike. Why not a fleet of them? And the most powerful telescope in the world. He could have anything, just by dreaming it. He could even have his mother back.

Suddenly Monica, who had reached the clifftop, came running toward them. She was pointing to the sky and shouting, but Matthew couldn't make out the words. And then his father grabbed her and put the knife to her throat.

"Give me the crystal, Matthew," his father repeated. "Give it to me or I'll kill her!"

Matthew saw the fear in Monica's eyes, and his heart raced. *I must stop him*, he thought.

It makes dreams come true.

Matthew felt anger swell inside him. Suddenly, he could see his father clearly, so small and insignificant. How easy it would be for Matthew to teach him a lesson. He could make his father see anything, feel anything Matthew dreamed up for him. And those dreams would become real … So easy … Righteous fury blazed in Matthew, and the crystal in his hand glowed, hot…

"No!"

The power to make all your dreams come true, Matthew thought. All of them. Even those from the darkest places in a person's heart.

And we all have a dark side…

This power is not for men.

Matthew noticed that Monica was still looking up at sky, and he turned and looked up, too.

"It's too late, Dad!" Matthew shouted triumphantly. "They've come!"

Three sets of bright lights drifted down out of the moonlit sky. Matthew smiled as he watched them descend. Then the smile faded from his face as, faintly at first, he heard the chop of rotor blades.

The three helicopters landed in a cloud of dust. In a flash, armed men appeared. One of them raised a rifle and fired, and Matthew's father spun to the ground, the knife flying from his hand.

"Dad!!" Matthew screamed. He ran and knelt by his father, who lay sprawled on his back, unconscious.

"Is he okay?" Monica asked as a group of armed men surrounded them.

A thin man with long dark hair crouched down beside Matthew.

"He'll be fine," the man said. "The bullet hit his shoulder. Hitting the ground knocked him out." The man stood up. "You must be Matthew Wilkes."

"Who are you?" Matthew asked, standing to face him.

"My name is Walker. This is Mr. Robinson," he said, gesturing to the young man standing next to him. "And that," Walker said, pointing at the crystal in Matthew's hand, "is what I came here for. Why don't you give that to me, young Mr. Wilkes?"

"No. You can't have it," Matthew said. "I won't give it to you. And you can't take it from me. I'd have to give it to you, and I won't."

Jack Walker's smile was warm and knowing, not frightening at all. They stared into each other's eyes for a moment. Then, in a sudden movement, like the lunge of a snake, Walker grabbed Matthew's arm and took the crystal.

"I'm afraid I must insist," Walker said quietly.

"But how ... " Matthew stammered.

Walker looked down at Matthew's father, shaking his head sadly. "Foolish man. And after your son came all this way to help you."

He turned back to face Matthew. "Your father was tempted by the power of this thing. But he also resisted it. All these years his two sides struggled to master it. He was trapped. But you, he guessed that you were special. That you ... " Walker's voice trailed off.

"I'm not sure I understand," Matthew said.

"It's not necessary that you understand. But I hope you can find it in your heart to forgive your father. It really isn't his fault, you know. The human condition."

Matthew thought for what seemed like a long time. "My father used the crystal to help Professor Schnabel build the ... " Matthew wasn't sure what to call it.

"I'd like to think of it as a dream catcher." Walker said. "But I suppose it's really more like a transmitter. To send a distress signal."

"To call them here. To take it back."

"Yes."

"But the other side of my father wanted the crystal for himself," Matthew said coldly. "That side called me. Because he thought he could control me."

"Yes. I'm sorry."

"The power is not for men," Matthew echoed.

Walker nodded. "That's why these few here have kept it a secret for so long."

"But how can you have it?"

"Because I don't want it."

"What are you going to do with it, then?"

142

"Why, nothing. Nothing at all," Walker said.

"What the—!" one of the agents said suddenly, and all eyes turned skyward.

At least a dozen more helicopters were descending like locusts.

Robinson turned to Walker. "I think our operation is about to be terminated," he said.

More armed men scrambled out of the copters as they touched down. But these men were dressed in military khaki.

"They can't stop him now," Matthew said. "He has the crystal."

"True, young man," Walker said. "And not only that, but if you'll take a second look ... " he said, gesturing skyward.

Matthew looked up, blinking, trying to focus on what he was seeing.

The sky seemed to be boiling; it looked like they were standing at the bottom of a vast cauldron, with a swirling, liquid sky above them. A billion tiny lights emerged from the center of the vortex, creating a billion spirals radiating outward. They traced an immense web in the sky, spinning faster and faster, dipping down toward them like the funnel of a tornado, and suddenly the air around them was a blaze of light, racing past them like a billion sparks in a wind tunnel, with a roar like an orchestra of jet engines.

Monica grabbed Matthew's arm; he put it around her and drew her close. They squinted against the brightness and put their hands over their ears.

And then suddenly, it was over.

In an instant the air became perfectly still, the night dead quiet, helicopter blades motionless. For a long time, no one on the top of the butte moved or said a word.

"What happened?" Matthew asked finally.

"Everything's so calm ..." Monica murmured.

"Where are they?" Matthew asked.

"They're here," Walker said. "If you'll just observe ..." Walker pointed toward the Hopi, all standing now on top of the butte. At first, Matthew saw nothing new in their appearance. But after a moment, he realized they wore the pure and simple smiles of children. The old man looked around with delight as if he were seeing everything for the first time. Walker approached him slowly, stopping a few feet away, as if waiting for permission to speak, there in the glare of the helicopter floodlights, surrounded by the dozens of soldiers and his own agents, all silent now, guns limp in their hands. Finally the old man looked at Walker and spoke with a voice not familiar to Matthew at all, an ancient voice, from somewhere far away, like an echo in the mountains. And Matthew knew that the man standing there was no longer just the old Indian mechanic. Now he was someone else, too, someone who had come from far away: The Elder Brother.

"An old friend of ours called us here," the Elder Brother said. "He sent us a message to come for him. Do you know where he is?"

"He died long ago, I am afraid," Walker said, and the Elder Brother nodded, as if the news had been expected. "But he left something for you." Walker extended his hand toward the Elder Brother, with the crystal cradled in his palm.

The Elder Brother looked at it for a long time, with a puzzled expression.

"You do not want it?" the Elder Brother asked at last.

"No, your friend thought it best that you take it back," Walker said. "And those through whom you are now speaking are the ones who kept it safe for you all this time."

"It is yours to keep, if you wish. We would not take it from you against your will."

"I know," Walker said. "That is why I give it."

The Elder Brother took the crystal from Walker's hand and suddenly began to juggle it back and forth between his hands, as if it were too hot for him to hold.

"Now I understand. It burns hot from so much hunger. So much desire." The Elder Brother nodded knowingly. "But now I am even more surprised you would give it up. Any of you would crave this thing, I think."

"Yes," Walker said.

The Elder Brother studied Walker, as if mulling this over.

"You are wise," the Elder Brother said at last.

"No, I'm not," Walker said. "I wish I were."

"We will leave now," the Elder Brother said.

"Wait!" Walker said. "Please, take me with you."

The Elder Brother looked deeply into Walker's eyes.

"Do I know you?" he asked. "Have we met before?"

"No," Walker answered.

"I seem to remember you," said the Elder Brother.

"Perhaps you remember what is yet to come," Walker said, and at this the Elder Brother smiled.

"Join us then. Do any of the others here wish to come?" The Elder Brother regarded the group standing silently around him. Matthew looked into the Elder Brother's eyes and felt the same trust he'd felt in the garden with him, when he was just an old mechanic, working the earth under the hot sun. Without thinking, Matthew stepped forward.

"Matt, what are you doing?" Monica said, grabbing his arm to stop him.

Matthew looked at Monica, then back at the Elder Brother. The Elder Brother's eyes seemed endlessly deep and comforting; they seemed to draw him in. Then Jack Walker stepped between Matthew and the Elder Brother.

"You've come all this way to find your father," Walker said. "Will you leave him now?" Matthew looked down at his father, still lying unconscious on the ground. And then he looked at Monica and saw that her eyes were filled with tears.

"No, I won't leave," Matthew said. "I'll stay."

Walker put his hand on Matthew's shoulder. "Goodbye, my boy," he said. Then he turned to Robinson. "Goodbye, Mr. Robinson," he said, and he and Robinson shook hands firmly.

"Others will leave tonight, won't they?" Robinson said. "All over the world?"

"Astute as always, Mr. Robinson," Walker said. "Many good people will leave tonight. But many others will choose to stay. Those who have things to do here, on this Earth, in this time." Walker glanced at Matthew. "Quite a story for the morning papers."

Walker approached the Elder Brother and the other Hopi. Suddenly the wind began to swirl again, and the bodies of Walker, the Elder Brother, and the rest of the Hopi became radiant, dissolving into another billion flecks of light. In a moment, their bodies were spread out across the sky and then vanished.

Those who remained on the top of the butte stood stunned, motionless in the calm night air.

"I would say the operation is terminated," Robinson said, looking around at the agents he'd arrived with and the soldiers who'd come to stop them. "I think I'd like to go home."

"Wow," said one of the soldiers. One by one they began to trickle back to the helicopters.

Monica cradled Matthew's face in her hands. "Look at me, Matt," she said. "Are you okay?"

A tear rolled down Matthew's cheek. He kissed her gently on the forehead.

Two soldiers lifted Matthew's father onto a stretcher.

146

"He'll be okay," one said to Matthew.

"Dad? Can you hear me?" Matthew said. His father stirred and opened his eyes.

"Matthew?" Jonathan Wilkes said.

"Yes, Dad, I'm here."

"I'm sorry, son. I'm so sorry," his father said, his face wet with tears.

"It's okay, Dad. It's okay now," Matthew said. His father's eyes closed, and he fell asleep. The soldiers carried the stretcher to one of the helicopters.

"I guess all fathers really are the same," Matthew said to Monica, his voice trembling. He felt like he'd lost his father a second time. His father was just a man now. As he always had been.

"You wanted to leave, didn't you?" Monica asked Matthew.

But Matthew knew he had to stay. The Old Man had chosen him. The Old Man was gone, the crystal was gone, but the Secret remained after all. The peaceful way. Everyone could learn this Secret. The way of peace becoming the way of all people.

"What do you think?" Matthew asked.

Matthew looked at her face; it seemed to glow in the last light of the full moon. She was more beautiful than he had ever seen her, more beautiful than anything he had ever seen.

"I think you're lonely." Monica said.

"I think I'm not," he said. Her eyes seemed to draw him in, liquid and luminous, and he could feel the whole world, the sun and the moon and the planets and all the multitude of stars and galaxies enveloped by them.

Everyone can learn this secret. Everyone can catch this dream. Everyone can make it come true.

They stood on the flat tabletop of the butte, far above the valley. And across the great desert, the sky in the east was glowing.

THE END

ACKNOWLEDGMENTS

Thanks to Anne Speyer for her keen editorial eye, to Suzanne Savoy for her insightful attention to detail, and to Noël Claro for her design skills and her wonderful enthusiasm.

And endless thanks and even more love to my wife Marianne for pretty much everything.